Conspiracy of Ravens

"Raven is my kind of people. Half hot-mess, half bad-ass, all awesome... the story was had plenty of humor, action and mystery rolled up in a nice paced story."   –Urban Fantasy Investigations

Nevermore

"The dramas, dangers, intrigue, and tension of NEVERMORE will have you glued to the pages, and when it is finished, Ms. McKenzie will have left you satisfied yet wanting more." –*Fresh Fiction*

The Night House

"From the very first page till the very end I was hooked on this book and read it in less than one day...it had everything you could want from a story romance, secrets, lies, suspense, surprises and more."   –Linda Tonis, Paranormal Romance Guild

Dangerous Dreams

"This new world promises to be an adventurous one full of snark, passion, thrills, romance, danger and wonderful characters and I can't wait to read the next one."   –*Stormy Vixen Reviews*

Dangerous Liaisons

"Loved this story and loved Raf and strong, stubborn Lara and I can't overlook Lara's dragon who brought humor to this story." – *Paranormal Romance Guild*

The Good Griffin

"THE GOOD GRIFFIN is as addictive as a double shot of espresso, only without any of the withdrawal symptoms." –*N. N. Light*

Books by J. C. McKenzie

Conspiracy of Ravens
Nevermore
Queen of Corvids
The Call of Corvids

Shift Happens
Beast Coast
Carpe Demon
Shift Work
Beast of All

Dangerous Dreams
Dangerous Liaisons
Dangerous Decisions

The Good Griffin

The Shucker's Booktique (out of print)
Be My Love (out of print)

The lighting in the room dimmed and the room cooled down. Bear lowered his arm. In front of him, in a glow of dazzling light, like a phoenix rising from its ashes, a woman dressed in ordinary jeans and a tank top stood with her hands on her hips and her feet shoulder width apart. The light highlighted her high cheekbones, smooth dark skin and shining platinum hair. Black eyes of the Underworld, eyes like his, studied him and her full red lips curled up with amusement. She was by far the most beautiful woman he'd ever seen.

His twin sister, Raven, had once told him his exterior was far prettier than who he was inside. She didn't normally talk to him like that, but she'd been especially pissed off at him for something. He couldn't remember what he'd done that particular time, but he deserved it. He always did. And despite her words being spoken in anger, she wasn't wrong.

Bear never lacked female attention. Women enjoyed his company and he enjoyed theirs. He put minimal, if any, effort into seducing a woman. He didn't need to. That wasn't arrogance, but experience. He never had to work for anything. He certainly didn't have to beg.

One mere second in this woman's company, and he wanted to crawl on the floor and grovel before her.

And that was all kinds of wrong.

Bjorn motherfucking Crawford did not beg.

"Who...who the fuck are you?" He pointed at her. "And get off my coffee table."

Praise for novels of J. C. McKenzie

Shift Happens

"SHIFT HAPPENS has excitement, intrigue and lots of danger. I love the whole cast of characters and how they played a part in the story"   *—Fresh Fiction*

Beast Coast

"I loved this book as much as the first. There are secrets, surprises, and all manner of supernaturals."   *—Paranormal Romance Guild*

Carpe Demon

"The story keeps the adrenaline pumping and spine tingling tension building throughout the story with well written scenes full of vivid details that capture the imagination and make it easy for the reader to become engrossed..." *—Literary Addicts Book Community*

Shift Work

"It's a terrific series and if you like supernatural reads, with a side of romance, the sort with solid and intense plots, gripping and very real dangers, hard choices, supernatural people some of whom can be selfish, cruel and bloodthirsty...You'll be hooked." *—Jeannie Zelos Book Reviews*

Beast of All

"This time out, J. C. McKenzie has outdone herself with high-velocity action, soul deep emotions and one of those finishes that you want to replay over and over!"   *—Tome Tender*

THE CALL OF CORVIDS

A RAVEN CRAWFORD SIBLING STORY, BOOK ONE

J. C. McKENZIE

COPYRIGHT INFORMATION

The Call of Corvids

Contact Information: jcmckenzie@jcmckenzie.ca

Cover Art: Eerilyfair Design
Raven artwork: Yauheniya Piatrouskaya
Raven in nest artwork: Chad Keith

Publishing History:
First JCM Publications Edition, 2020

ISBN: 978-1-9992394-6-6 (print)
ISBN: 978-1-9992394-7-3 (ebook)

To Mirren Hogan,
The house may be gone, but the home is in the heart.
I'm wishing you the strength to rebuild.

Chapter One

"There are a lot of mysterious things about boats, such as why anyone would get on one voluntarily."

~ *P. J. O'Rourke*

Bear Crawford tucked his chin and pumped his arms. Stretching out his legs, he quickened his pace. Faster. He needed to run faster. His footsteps echoed down the dark alley while the spring moon laughed at him.

The guards grunted somewhere farther down the alley. He didn't dare look.

Adrenaline raced through Bear's veins and his heart

punched against his breastbone. He clutched the stolen book in one hand and kept running. His leather jacket squeaked with each stride.

Almost there. The intensifying smell of ocean cheered him on.

A raven swooped down from her perch on the building's ledge and hovered beside him. Her energy pinged against his. Though most birds couldn't communicate more than a word or two, they often shared images and feelings with him. This one sent visions of birds playing in the air flows. Tasha. Though she looked no different than any other female raven, he'd know this bird and her mischievous energy anywhere. She followed him like a shadow.

Not now, he told her. Not ever. He didn't have that kind of talent, but she didn't understand that. She kept sensing his corvid energy and assumed he could shift into a bird.

The sleek raven clicked at him before flapping her wings and taking off into the night. If only he could join her. Instead, he rounded the corner and pushed his body harder. Where had these guards come from? He'd scouted the location for weeks and studied the schematics of the building until his eyes crossed. He must've tripped some sort of silent alarm—one installed after the company updated the latest security plan on their internal website.

Bear gnashed his teeth. The black material covering his face scratched his skin. He wanted to tear it off and feel the fresh air, but he couldn't risk it. Of course, if he had his sister's power, he'd already be free.

Bear grimaced. It wasn't Raven's fault she inherited more magic from their absentee biological father. Just as it wasn't her fault Bear hadn't been around much lately. But now was not the time to dwell or drown in guilt.

The thundering footsteps behind him drifted farther away. He created more distance between himself and his pursuers. That expensive gym membership finally paid off.

One more turn.

Bear rounded the last corner toward the docks.

He almost skidded to a halt. One of the guards waited for him, red-faced and panting by the entrance of the docks. The guard spotted him and braced in a ready position more commonly seen on rugby players than security for hire. How in the Underworld did he get here first?

Bear growled and charged ahead. Rugby happened to be one of Bear's favourite sports.

The guard—Red, for the face—narrowed his eyes and lunged at him.

Bear sidestepped and flung out his hand—straight-arming Red. The guard's heavy body slammed against Bear's hand, but he locked his elbow and held Red off. He cradled the stolen book under his other arm like a rugby ball.

The guard swiped and grabbed at empty air, unable to get a grip on Bear's clothes or bring him down. The guard lunged forward, throwing his considerable weight at Bear.

With sheer determination and muscle memory, Bear danced out of Red's reach. He gripped the stolen property. Good. He still had possession.

Red grunted and fell face-first into the pavement behind him. His body smacked the ground with a loud thud. Without breaking stride, Bear ran down the ramp to the docks.

Loosely tethered to the end was a cheap tin boat he'd purchased as a backup plan. Good thing, too, or he'd be dead.

Footsteps pounded behind him.

He wasn't free yet.

With a flying leap, Bear jumped in the boat, pulled the rope and let the natural momentum push the vessel from the dock. He straightened to smugly smile at the guards, and—

Fuck!

One of the guards jumped from the dock, aiming his body straight at Bear's. He barrelled into Bear, and they crashed into the boat.

Oomph.

Bear's head smacked the side of the vessel. His ears rang. Before he could right himself, a fist smashed into his side.

Bear grunted and tensed his ab muscles to brace for the next fist. And the next. He needed to move, not get pummeled by some random guard. With a deep breath, he dropped the artifact, pushed off the bottom of the boat and jabbed out with his fist. His knuckles slammed into the guard's neck.

The guard gurgled and reeled back, stumbling with the movement of the unsteady boat. Salt spray sloshed over the metal side. The vessel had drifted farther from the docks. Hopefully, far enough to discourage any other guards from joining them.

Bear got to his feet, the boat swaying back and forth even more. If they weren't careful, the vessel would capsize. Even if Bear survived the frigid and gelatinous waters, poisoned from years of turmoil between regs and fae, the stolen book and his source of income wouldn't.

The guard scrambled to regain his footing. He squared off with a snarl, telegraphing his intent. His weight shifted to his toes. The guard was getting desperate, he'd put everything into his next move.

Bear wasn't a lethal fae warrior, but he benefitted from the corvid essence running through his veins. Like the birds he could communicate with, he read people very well.

The guard lunged forward.

Bear stomped down with his right foot with all his weight.

The boat rocked to the side and the guard stumbled.

Now was his chance. Bear struck out with his fist, contacting the man's face. The momentum, with the boat listing, sent the guard tumbling over the side. His body smacked the surface of the ocean and salt water sprayed Bear's body and face mask.

Bear panted, wanting nothing more than to sit down

and catch his breath, but he was too close to shore and a dock full of angry guards.

He reached down, and gripped the cord for the engine. The guard in the water gurgled and latched onto the side of the boat. The vessel listed. Bear stumbled. The congealed depths of murky ocean loomed.

Bear kicked out, stomping on the guard's fingers, crushing them and righting himself. Nope. He wouldn't be falling over the side and joining the guard for a sludgy ocean bubble bath tonight.

The man screamed and fell back into the water with a splash. A plume of foul ocean air hit Bear's face and he shuddered. If the guard focused on swimming back to the dock, he'd survive. Hopefully, he chose life over making Bear's job more difficult.

Bear pulled the cord and the engine sputtered to life. The oddly comforting smell of gasoline pumped into the air.

The guards left behind on the dock shouted obscenities about Bear's mother, while their comrade flailed in the water a few feet away and tried to shoot Bear down with a death stare. Neither of these things prevented Bear from slipping into the night in a cheap tin can of a boat.

He'd been lucky. If any of those guards had been armed...If any of them had been fae...

Bear shook his head. He didn't get paid to complete easy jobs.

Tasha swooped down from the night sky and

perched on the bow.

"Hey, girl."

She cocked her head at him and clicked.

After he was far enough away from security cameras and prying eyes, he pulled the balaclava from his head. His black hair stood straight up and sweat had dried to his face. The cool wind flowing over the still waters of Burrard inlet rushed by, a refreshing reminder that he'd survived another job.

And he was one step closer to his goal.

Chapter Two

"People who enjoy meetings should not be in charge of anything."

~ *Thomas Sowell*

Born as Bjorn Crawford, Bear never lived up to the fancy name his mom carefully selected for him, but he found success in other things. Mainly stealing stuff and living a life of crime. That hadn't been his original goal, but after trying, and failing, to make a living the honest way, he focused on just making a living. Period.

Bear pulled up the collar of his leather jacket and

hunched his shoulders against the bitter breeze. Shockingly cold for a late spring night, the air drifting off the ocean surface had been refreshing at first but had since turned frigid and bone-numbing. Bear couldn't wait to get home, crank the heat and cuddle with his cat. Instead, he stood in an empty parking lot on the North Shore waiting for the client to show up so he could hand over the "artifact" and collect payment.

Normally, Eli handled this crap.

Eli was his contact from the guild of thieves that resided in the Underworld—a dark fae-operated realm that used to be closed off from the Mortal Realm by a magical barrier. That barrier crashed down when a bunch of scientists fucked around with stuff they didn't quite understand. A whole lot of invasions, servitude and death followed, but eventually things settled into an uneasy truce with everyone more or less staying on their respective sides and playing by the rules. Mostly.

Now, magicless humans, known as regs, cohabitated the damaged Mortal Realm alongside supernatural beings native to Earth who, due to circumstances created by the barrier collapse, no longer hid their powers and abilities. Most regs desperately wished for things to return to "normal" and clung to a misplaced belief that restoring the barrier and ridding the world of fae would somehow magically make all their problems go away. It didn't matter that the barrier collapse happened generations ago. It didn't matter that extensive research and trials had failed to reconstruct anything remotely similar to the magical barrier. And it certainly didn't matter that they had no personal experience with the dream they so fanatically craved.

Bear wasn't holding out or wishing for a new shiny world. He certainly wasn't waiting. What was the point? The faepocalypse happened before he was born and this was his reality. Life was too short. Things would never go back to "normal" and sitting around hoping wouldn't change that. Regs and weak half-fae like himself needed to adapt to survive.

Though Bear knew working with and for the fae held more of a future than sticking his head in the sand like a delusional ostrich, a healthy dose of caution for the fatherland and fae kept him honest and kept him alive. He didn't venture into the Other Realms often. He avoided them. Mom's constant nagging and excessive warnings throughout his childhood made up the structural fibre of his very being. Besides, he didn't like the feeling of potent magic against his small stash of power. Vulnerability and weakness weren't his jam. He rarely placed himself in a position where he was out of his element.

Luckily, Eli travelled back and forth and maintained an outpost for contracts in the Mortal Realm. Fat lot of good it did Bear right now, though. Apparently, the client wanted a direct handover, which always carried more risk. Eli hadn't sounded pleased with the stipulation, either, but Bear couldn't tell whether Eli was insulted at the implication he was untrustworthy, or pissed off at the loss of half his handler fee.

"Artifact," Bear grunted. With a worn cover, dog-eared corners, and a slightly musty smell, the book looked more like one of his sister's old notebooks from school.

At first, Bear worried he'd stolen the Murdoch Manual—the infamous notes of the lead physicist from the group responsible for "accidentally" tearing down the magical barrier separating the Mortal Realm from the Other Realms. Stealing the coveted manual carried a death sentence. Despite taking on risky jobs, Bear didn't have a death wish. He was relieved to read a different name scrawled in fancy handwriting on the cover.

Lindh. Only a few people read handwriting these days, but Bear was one of them. Had the client banked on him not reading cursive?

Bear flipped the book open, shuddered and quickly slammed it shut. Ugh. Math.

Bear's phone vibrated in his pocket. He tucked the book under his arm and pulled out the phone. If this was Eli calling to tell him the client had changed the drop location or time, he was going to get angry. He'd already lost feeling in his toes and fingertips. Even Tasha had abandoned him to find warmer shelter.

Bear glanced at the screen. Unknown caller. He punched the green accept button with his thumb and brought the phone to his ear. "Hello?"

"Bear! You lying piece of shit," a woman shrieked.

Bear winced. "Monica?"

A scary silence answered him. Well, crap. That

hadn't been the right thing to say.

"It's Janice," she hissed, low and scary.

Oh, right. Janice. Memories of passionate nights rolling around in his bed in a tangle of sheets and limbs brought a smile to his lips. "Janice."

"Don't you purr at me, you two-timing asswipe."

Huh? "What's wrong?"

"You used me and moved on to some whore named Monica. That's what's *wrong*."

"Hang on a minute—"

"You just go through women, moving on from one to the next like you're some sort of cock carousel."

"Cock carousel." Bear repeated. That was a new one.

"And everyone's had a ride, apparently."

Bear took a deep breath, unsure of where to start. He didn't really deserve this, but he needed to deescalate the situation, "Janice. I'm sorry that you're upset."

Janice screamed.

Bear winced. Okay. That wasn't the right thing to say, either.

"Don't even," Janice said. "That's not a true apology."

Bear sighed. She was right, of course. He used the same words with his siblings when he wanted to see them turn red. "You're right, but I'm not sure what I'm apologizing for. I enjoyed our time together, and thought you did, too. When we first met, I made it very clear anything between us would be temporary. I told you I was looking for something casual. I'm not into serious relationships. If I recall correctly, you were okay with that. You were rebounding from some asshole and wanted companionship without any strings attached. I don't understand why you're upset with me or how I wronged you. What changed?"

"I changed."

"Oh." Well, he couldn't really be blamed for that, could he?

The bushes on the opposite side of the empty parking lot rustled.

"Look, Janice. I'd love to talk more, but—"

"Don't do that. Don't push me out. We need to talk about this now."

"Why? What could possibly change now? Why do we need to talk about this at all?" She'd already called him an impressive range of names and clearly communicated her anger and dissatisfaction of how things ended between them. What more could she want?

"I want more."

"Hell of a way to ask for it." Bear flinched.

Janice sucked in a breath, probably readying herself to give him a verbal lashing.

Crap. That was definitely not the right thing to say. Dick move. He wasn't wrong, but...

A man emerged from the bushes on the far side of the parking lot and stepped into the light.

"This isn't a good time, Janice."

More shrieking erupted from his phone. He cringed

and hung up. He never intentionally hurt women. He was up front and honest. Bear must be missing something in his communications, though, because he found himself in this position more often than not. He had no intention of changing his ways or what he wanted, he just wished women believed him when he said he didn't want a committed relationship. How could he have anything long term or meaningful?

He sighed, tucked the phone back in his pocket and walked out to meet the client.

Tasha croaked in a nearby tree and her energy pinged against Bear's. He smiled, glad she had returned. He ignored the dark Other energy within begging to come out and play. Instead, he focused on the person in the otherwise empty parking lot.

Wearing a cheap suit, the skinny man looked more like a down-and-out accountant or public defense lawyer, not a criminal mastermind or a purveyor of stolen goods. He was probably just a lackey acting as a go between.

"Let's see it," the man said as he got closer. His thin whiney voice rubbed Bear the wrong way.

Bear shrugged off the grating effect. He couldn't afford to react to silly things. Not when he needed to look for more dangerous indicators. The guy hadn't done anything wrong. Yet.

Bear pulled the book from under his arm and held it up for the man to see the cover and read the name scrawled across it.

The man's shoulders relaxed, and he let out a long

breath. He stepped forward to take the book.

Bear backed up and shook his head. "Let's see the payment."

"Your fee isn't cheap." The man pulled out an envelope from an inside pocket of his ill-fitting jacket, opened the flap and tipped it toward Bear so he could see the contents. Bear counted the amount quickly without seeing the faces—the one benefit of Canadian currency resembling board game money

Bear nodded and the man closed the envelope.

"Cheap, no, but this was a dangerous job."

The man scowled. "Not as dangerous as my associate. He is most eager to review this book."

Bear shrugged. He didn't care.

It was human nature to want to fill the silence. In Bear's line of work, he never offered more information than necessary. This man was an inexperienced criminal. He hadn't learned the art of ignoring that "fill-in-the-blank" urge yet.

"Let's do this," Bear said.

He held out the journal with one hand. The man reached out and grabbed the notebook, but Bear didn't release it. He flapped his fingers on his other hand for the envelope. "The money."

Instead of placing the payment in Bear's open hand, the client dropped it. The full envelope smacked the concrete.

Motherfucker.

"Oops." The man didn't sound sorry.

Bear glanced down at his money.

The man reached into his jacket, his face gleaned with sweat.

Bear froze, his scalp prickling. His heart stopped. Time slowed.

The man pulled a gun from his jacket. Before he aimed and pulled the trigger, a giant-ass bird swooped down from the trees with a shrill croak and sunk its talons into the man's face.

That's not Tasha.

The client shrieked and swatted at the raven, trying to bat the black bird away and stop it from tearing at his face.

Huh.

Bear hadn't called for help. Interesting. He stood for half a second and studied the attack bird before shaking his head. He could dwell on the inconsistencies of his dark fae power later. He needed to get out of here first. With another glance to ensure the client was still occupied with saving his eyeballs, Bear crouched down and picked up the envelope. Double checking it held the correct amount, he pocketed the money and straightened.

The client still stumbled around nearby, flailing his arms. He'd dropped the gun in an attempt to defend himself from the tenacious bird. It lay on the ground a few feet away.

I'll take that, thank you.

Bear reached down and plucked the weapon from the cold pavement. He had no intention of shooting the client or keeping the gun for his personal collection, but he didn't want to leave it for the man to shoot him in the back either.

Bear checked the safety before shoving the gun into his waistband and pulling his shirt and jacket over the grip to hide it. He'd dispose of the weapon later.

When Bear approached the client, the raven released the man's face and croaked a "fuck you" before disappearing into the night.

The client groaned and staggered. He had various scratches and cuts on his face and hands, but nothing requiring medical assistance. He would heal in a few weeks.

Bear didn't give the man time to recuperate. He kicked him as hard as he could in the knee. The client cried out. His leg buckled and he bent over in pain.

Bear leaned down. "Think twice before you try to cross a thief again." He drove his fist into the man's face.

The client crumpled to the ground, knocked out but still breathing. Probably better than he deserved considering he'd come to the drop-off tonight intent on killing Bear.

Bear's fist throbbed, but the discomfort was worth it. He'd make sure Eli knew this guy tried to double cross him. The guild wouldn't take another contract from him and if they decided to really take exception, they'd place a price on his head.

Bear glanced at the notebook on the ground. Something about it called to him. He could take it with him. He had every right. But just as something lured him in, something else about the journal set him on edge. If he took it, there would be a ripple effect. He didn't want to spend his life looking over his shoulder.

He picked up the notebook and dropped it on the client. A low keening sound emitted from the man but he remained face down on the pavement.

The phone in Bear's pocket vibrated as he turned to leave. He pulled it free and answered as he stepped into the safety of the forest. He followed the hiking trail and made his way to the car. "This isn't really a good time, Janice."

Tasha swooped down and landed on his shoulder. Her talons dug into his leather jacket. She head-butted his cheek and he reached up to scratch her neck.

"I've been called many things before, but not that." Eli's deep voice sounded amused. "How'd the drop off go?"

"He tried to kill me."

"As expected, then?" Eli's tone was dry.

And that was what pissed off Bear. He knew the man would try something. He had expected it. Yet, the man's ordinary appearance, whiney voice and inexperience lulled Bear into enough complacency that he'd caught Bear off-guard. Rookie mistake.

Now Bear wanted to go home, get warm and order takeout. He also had to feed the cat before she pooped in his shoes.

"Yeah," he said, answering Eli even though his handler hadn't asked a question. "What's up?"

"I have another job for you."

Chapter Three

"Do not underestimate your abilities. That is your boss's job."

~ *Unknown*

B ear stepped into a sparsely decorated office, and instantly wanted to punch someone in the face. He never trusted money, or, more specifically, the people who had a lot of it. He had no problem with the dollar bills on their own and spent the majority of his adult life trying to make as much money as possible. This probably made him a bit of a hypocrite, but having a consistent hate-on for the wealthy made it easier for Bear to steal from the rich.

The penthouse office in downtown Vancouver with floor-to-ceiling windows screamed money. Yet, no name plaques or business decals decorated the door or hallway, or even the front of the building.

An illegal business.

Perfect.

They might be his client today, but tomorrow they might be his target. Thieves owed loyalty only to themselves. And in Bear's case, his family.

A receptionist who looked more like a plastic mannequin than a human, with a fancy hairdo and painted face, stared out from behind an empty counter with the shiny surface. No business cards. No papers. No printer that he could see.

A pop-up business. Too bad. He'd continue to note the security details for future reference, just in case, but this "business" would most likely be gone tomorrow.

All the usual warning bells went off in his head and like always, he ignored them.

Eli had kept him busy these last few months since the botched book deal, but none of the jobs had been financially lucrative. The payout promised for this job would allow Bear to finally step out of the shady world of criminals and start his own legal business where he'd make his own name, be his own boss, and finally have something he could be proud to show his family. He wanted to prove he wasn't useless.

He could've worked as a private investigator for his

stepfather, of course, but he never would've raised enough capital to branch out on his own, he'd always be that guy leaching off his parents, and he'd have to take orders from someone else.

He didn't dislike his stepdad. Quite the opposite. He respected the man for his principles and for stepping in to help raise Bear and his twin sister when other men would've run. Bear couldn't work for Terry because he wanted to prove to his stepfather he could be his own man.

The pristine counter reflected his face when he stepped forward. "I have a three-fifteen appointment." He didn't offer a name. He didn't need one. Real names in this business were just as dangerous as the clients.

The receptionist blinked and nodded once. Her fingers flew across the screen of a tablet on the ledge behind the counter. Beside the tablet rested a coffee in a takeaway cup with the name "Rybekka" typed onto a sticky label underneath the name of the actual order, which was too long and too complicated for Bear to give a shit. Coffee was just coffee.

Bear cringed, half-expecting his twin sister, Raven, to leap out from behind the counter to smack him for the coffee-blasphemy. His shoulders dropped and a mix of relief and sadness passed through him. Bear missed his twin, but it was probably for the best that his loud-mouthed, prone-to-disaster sister wasn't here.

Beside the receptionist's takeaway cup was a romance novel. She must be bored out of her mind.

"Right this way." She pushed away from the desk and stood. The tight pencil skirt made him think of a teetering top hat. That made no sense, of course, the woman was beautiful and didn't resemble an old-school childhood toy in any way. She took short steps in tall heels to walk around the counter and extended her arm toward the hallway.

Bear nodded, pulled his shoulders back and followed the receptionist. Would she fall over? How did she defy gravity like that? A security camera tracked his movement, picking up the field of view where the other camera outside the elevator left off.

Rybekka sidled up to large double doors. Though she was beautiful, she looked ridiculous taking short little steps on her stilts. A lot of men would drool over her beauty, but not Bear. She looked as though she'd break like fine china. Pretty to look at, but a pain to handle.

Bear wasn't a rough guy, but he liked capable, hardier women. Women who didn't cave to this plastic version of beauty.

The receptionist stepped back and plastered on a fake smile with perfect teeth.

If he felt anything for this woman, it was sadness. He'd hate to find either of his sisters dolled up and prancing around like this. Maybe this woman didn't have a choice. Maybe she did what she did to pay the bills. And maybe, just maybe, she enjoyed her work and took pride in how she looked, and Bear was just a judgemental asshole.

Probably the latter.

Bear sighed. Maybe he should stop dissecting the internal motivations of a receptionist he had no intention of trying to get to know better and focus instead on the bigger issue. The more dangerous issue.

"Thank you," he said and pulled open the door to the right. A red light blinked above the door—a motion sensor embedded in the door frame. Slick.

Rybekka dipped her head and teetered back to the front desk, while Bear slipped into the office and let the large door close behind him. In less than a second, Bear took a snap shot of the room, committed it to memory and analyzed the results.

A large executive desk sat in the middle, sandwiched by two office chairs worth more than his car. Aside from the furniture and fairy filter, the otherwise barren room lacked any unique or worthwhile sensory details. Sterile.

The giant office reminded him of an operating room without any equipment, patients, or hospital staff.

Okay, so maybe not quite like an operating room, but it had the same clinical feel.

Someone had set a fairy filter on one of the floor-to-ceiling windows, preventing the less-than-desirable stink of the neighbourhood from entering, letting in only the sweet smells of summer.

Bear took pride in evaluating his surroundings and how well he blended in. His leather jacket and ripped jeans stood out. The scruff on his face stood out. His very presence stood out like a dark stain on a white shirt. Even if he wore a stolen suit, he'd stand out in this room.

A tall man in a business suit stood facing the floor-to-ceiling windows with his back to the room. Making a statement without words. He couldn't possibly be this cliché.

"Mr. Crawford. Please take a seat." The man's low rumbling voice filled the room.

Bear eyed the office chair with its sleek black leather upholstery without a single crease from wear. Had this client dropped a couple of grand on office chairs just to furnish the fake office for this meeting? Amateur. They could've met in a pub, an alley, or a coffee shop. These pretenses were unnecessary. At least for Bear.

Bear didn't typically meet clients. That was why he had a handler. Eli normally gathered the particulars. This client had demanded to meet with Bear personally instead of allowing the handler to act as a go-between. Along with the office set-up and rent-a-model receptionist, this meant the client was a control freak. He needed to control every aspect of this meeting down to the very furniture they sat on.

"I'll stand, thank you," Bear said. *Control that.*

The man turned around, arrogance and power evident in his stern features. His expensive suit had been custom tailored to fit his large frame, but no amount of clean lines could hide his powerful build. Annoyance streaked across his expression.

Yup. Control freak. Bear nailed it.

The man's dark energy vibrated off his skin and travelled in waves across the room to push against Bear.

Bear stiffened. Too much dark energy. Fuck. The client was a dark fae lord. The power punching Bear's senses right now confirmed he was at a severe disadvantage if the meeting turned confrontational. Bear wouldn't walk out of here alive if the client took exception to anything he said or did. So, basically, he was fucked.

If he had to bet money, this guy was another bored bastard who'd slipped past the barrier to try his hand at "playing reg," a despicable practice where dark fae pranced around, pretending to be regular mortals, while enticing the very people they pretended to be into making deals they couldn't possibly keep. The client wasn't even particularly good at it. He only half-ass shielded his power.

Dark fae got their name because they hailed from the Underworld. Though they had a wide range of physical traits from heights, hair colour, skin tone and build, they were all attractive and had potent magic. But the main way to identify a dark fae was their black irises, which bled out to cover the whites of their eyes when they experienced intense emotion or accessed their power. Eyes of the Underworld, like his.

Apprehension gripped his gut. His muscles tensed and he looked for possible exits. This wasn't the first job to trigger the fight or flight response, and it probably wasn't the last, either. Mortals weren't welcoming to the fae. Did the client not worry about the repercussions of exposure? Or was it simply the fae was so powerful, Bear and whomever he may or may not report to didn't factor into his concerns at all?

"It's unusual for a client to ask for a face-to-face meeting over a contract," Bear said.

The man smiled slowly and walked over to the desk. "I don't wish for the guild to know the particulars of this job."

That actually made sense. Going through the guild held a certain risk for clients. It could end up a double-edged sword. Bear nodded to concede the client's point. "Let's discuss the task, then."

The man pulled out a matching office chair on his side of the barren mahogany desk and waved at the other chair for a second time before sitting down.

Bear swallowed a growl and sat on the stiff unused leather.

"I require you to procure an artifact from a secure compound."

Bear nodded again. This information had been included in the contract along with the offered payment. That was about it, but the latter part of the contract was enough to entice Bear.

"Who owns this compound and exactly how secure is it?" he asked.

"The compound is owned by a merchant of sorts. Not big in the game."

"Does this merchant have a name?"

The client shook his head and reached into his jacket to pull out a white business card. He placed it on the desk and slid the card across the smooth surface.

Bear plucked the card off the desk. A number was embossed in magnetic gray on one side. He flipped it over. On the back, in elegant handwriting someone had written an address. Bear sighed. He'd prefer the owner's name and security details, but this was enough to find out more. After all, it was a part of his job to find out this information, and even if the client provided security details, Bear always double and triple checked. He never trusted clients to pass along accurate information.

Bear pocketed the card and returned his attention to the man. "And the artifact?"

"The Klee-uhv Suleesh."

Bear raised his eyebrow. A fae name, presumably for a fae artifact. "How do you spell that?"

"C-l-a-í-o-m-h S-o-l-a-i-s."

Ugh. Fucking fae words with their weird fae pronunciations. He knew he should've taken fae in school instead of Canadian French. He mentally spelled the word out in his head repeatedly, training his brain to remember by repetitive thoughts. Claíomh Solais. Something to do with light. "What does it translate to?"

"White glaive of light."

"A sword?" Bear frowned. He didn't often steal weapons. Those jobs tended to go sideways fast.

The client shook his head and reached into his jacket pocket again. He pulled out a phone, tapped the screen and swiped. When he found what he was looking for, he paused, hesitating before turning the phone so Bear could see the screen.

Bear leaned forward. Definitely not a sword. A box. A little wooden box with intricately carved designs on its sides. "Any chance I can get a copy of this photo?"

"None."

Bear glanced up at the cold tone. The man's stony expression startled him. Bear's stomach sunk. As if hearing a jail door slam shut, Bear knew, just knew, he'd somehow passed the point of no return for this contract. The man's face and body language spelled death. Bear had seen the picture and if he backed out now, somehow, someway, he'd end up floating in the gelatinous Burrard Inlet.

Bear swallowed. He didn't need a copy of the photo. The artifact had already left an impression on his memory, anyway. He doubted he could forget it now. What he needed was a way out. Out of this job, out of this man's office, out of this building. There wasn't one. Not one that left him alive. He pushed forward instead. "Do I need any special equipment or instructions to handle the artifact?"

Something flashed in his client's cold gaze—a gleam, an instantaneous moment of emotion. This man wanted the Claíomh Solais. And he wanted it badly. "There's no special handling requirements for the artifact itself. However, be warned, the moment you touch the Claíomh Solais it will most likely trigger a silent alarm."

"Alarms can be—"

"Not this one. Plan to get out of there right away. A lodestone. A portal. Something. Move quickly. Get to a safe place and once there, draw these on the walls." The man reached into his inside pocket again—making Bear wonder what else this man had stashed in there— and pulled out an aged piece of paper. He slid it across the desk like he had the card.

Bear glanced down at the paper. "Runes?"

"They will trap the artifact in the room and prevent anyone from portalling to you."

Bear studied the runes again. "When do you want it?"

"By the end of the month."

Bear looked up from examining the runes. "That doesn't give me a lot of time to plan and carry out the task."

"And the price I'm willing to pay for this contract compensates for the rush job, wouldn't you agree?"

Bear ground his teeth. Yes. It certainly did. The price tag did more than adequately compensate and was just what Bear desperately needed.

"And you know it's at this location?"

"I'm certain of it. The merchant keeps it in a secure vault."

Bear tapped the table by the paper with the runes scribbled on it. He'd have to practice drawing these things. Artwork wasn't one of his specialties.

Well, not making art. Stealing it was another story.

"Do we have a deal?" the man asked, casually, as if asking Bear if he planned to watch the game, or if he wanted some tea. As if Bear saying no wouldn't result in anything other than a polite farewell.

Every alarm bell rang in his head this time. Like a cacophony of seven year olds armed with recorders. Everything in his body said, "No." But Bear didn't get where he was today by running from tough or dangerous jobs. He took risks. Calculated ones. This man may try to double cross him, but he had a plan for that.

Bear stood and nodded, not officially voicing consent, which the fae could and would use against him. "I'll be in touch."

Something flashed across the man's face as he stood. "One more thing."

Bear groaned internally. "Yes?"

"Don't open it."

Wasn't planning on it.

"It will be your death."

Well, fuck.

Chapter Four

"I did surveillance a lot, which sounds exciting, but it never was."

~ *Miranda Lambert*

Bear leaned back on the bench surrounded by the warm afternoon heat and the slightly off scent in the air. The mortal realm hadn't fared well after the barrier collapse. Years of fighting, biological warfare, pollution and neglect had turned the once-beautiful environment to near ruin. Only magic borrowed, stolen or purchased from Otherkind kept the rot contained inside a perimeter of the Lower

Mainland while preventing an outright collapse of the ecosystem. Hopefully with time, the earth would heal itself.

Tasha perched on the bench's backrest a few feet away and basked in the sun, indifferent to their less-than-ideal surroundings. Like all corvids, she adapted well. They had that in common.

He forced his muscles to relax despite the unease crawling along his spine. This "secure compound" was a fucking fortress. Two external parameters. Multiple guards. Overlapping shifts and watches.

Bear scowled and checked his phone. He'd set up a number of small security cameras around the compound. Now, he could sit in a nearby park and watch from multiple vantage points.

The guards wouldn't pose the biggest obstacle. The dark energy radiating from the gates and the security system panel at the main entrance indicated the owner relied on magic and technology in addition to manpower to guard whatever he hoarded inside.

His mind flashed to the memory of the small wooden box. Seemed like a lot of effort to guard a chunk of dead tree. Exactly what was in the box? What else did the compound contain?

A couple of crows swooped in and landed on the backrest of the city bench. One hopped over to Bear. Tasha squawked a warning, the bird equivalent of "back off my man," but like all corvids drawn to his energy, they ignored her.

"Hey boy." Bear reached out and scratched the back

of the nearest crow's neck while he flicked between the different camera feeds.

How in the Underworld would he pull this off?

The other crow flapped her wings and maneuvered around Bear to land on his shoulder. When he didn't immediately drop his phone or stop scratching her friend, she head-butted his cheek. Bear chuckled and reached over to scratch her.

The other crow squawked and puffed out his neck feathers.

Tasha croaked, clearly unhappy about the entire situation—how dare other birds get attention and not her.

Bear ignored them all and continued to study the compound. If he focused hard enough on the details, he might succeed with shushing the concerns rampaging in his mind. Whomever owned this complex was loaded. Sure, merchants spent a large portion of their profits on security, but Bear had never seen anything quite like this before.

The technology would most likely be state of the art. His normal passcodes and mediocre hacking skills wouldn't cut it. He needed a tech upgrade.

Luckily, he knew a guy.

More crows called out from the surrounding trees and landed on the bench, his lap and shoulders. At one time in his life, more than thirty would've flocked to him by now.

Cut it out, you guys, he told the birds. *I need space*.

The crows cawed and clicked at him, head-butting

and preening for attention.

This was why he had a cat.

Not that he hated birds. He loved them. He loved all animals. He'd pet a crocodile if it wouldn't bite his hand off.

But any bird from the corvid family, like crows and ravens, were drawn to his Other energy. It was a passive effect of his power. If he sat around in any place long enough, he'd draw any corvids in the area to him. Even with the dwindling numbers, without a cat to act as a natural deterrent, he'd constantly be draped with birds. That wasn't just a minor annoyance. He'd spend all his time cleaning up bird shit and his professional career would be ruined.

More birds flocked to him and the cars zooming down the busy road slowed down to gawk.

Not good.

He probably looked like one of those statues at a park that someone liberally sprinkled with birdseed.

He shrugged the birds off. *Space, please.*

The birds squawked and with a flap of wings and a flurry of feathers, they launched from the bench and his body. Even Tasha took off. They didn't fly far. Instead, the birds perched on nearby trees and powerlines waiting for their opportunity to swoop in for more attention the moment he dropped his guard.

A large raven remained on the bench, its long talons clutching the metalwork of the bench's backrest. Tasha squawked a complaint somewhere in the nearby trees. Her jealous energy pinged against his own.

Bear glared at the bird, who was by far the largest fucking raven he'd ever seen.

The bird cocked his head and blinked his beady eyes at him.

"Fine. You can stay."

The other raven clicked and if Bear didn't know any better, he'd swear the raven laughed at him.

Chapter Five

"If you have any trouble sounding condescending, find a Unix user to show you how it's done."

~ *Scott Adams*

Text scrolled down an extra-wide monitor, stark, emotionless and an absolute contrast to the red-headed computer geek sitting in his office chair. Bear's brother, Mike, stared at him as if he'd spontaneously sprouted a second head.

"Come on, Mikey," Bear said, careful not to touch anything in this cesspool his younger brother insisted on living in. The sooner Mike conquered his inner fox's desire to mark and claim territory with his body odour, the sooner everyone remotely connected to Mike would rejoice.

"You want a breaker box for *all* high-end security panels?" Mike double blinked at him. Though he had red hair instead of black, a slight runner's build and a different biological father, at times like this, especially when Mike scowled at him, Bear swore he looked at a mirror image of his younger self.

Raven, their sister, was adamant Mike would end up with Terry's lean frame instead of taking after Bear's bulkier figure, but Bear wasn't so convinced.

Mike was only nineteen and would start his second year in the nearby university's computer engineering program this fall. He spent the majority of his time in front of a screen. If Mike spent a little more time with weights, and a little less time gaming, he'd bulk up. But Mikey never seemed particularly concerned with his appearance. He marched to his own drum, and there was nothing wrong with that. At least not in Bear's opinion, and he'd punch anyone who said otherwise. The only people allowed to mock Mike and make his life miserable were their sisters and Bear.

Workouts were the least of Mike's concerns. If Terry ever found out his baby boy provided his older brother with illegal materials to commit crimes, he'd lose it. Terry was a private investigator who conducted business by the book. He might actually burst out of his khaki pants and polo shirt if he found out what Mike was up to "for fun."

"Does Rayray know you're visiting?" Mike asked. "She'll be pissed she missed you."

Bear shook his head. "Isn't she out on surveillance anyway?"

"Yeah. Mom and Dad are with Juni at some volleyball summer camp. You really picked your time." Mike tapped his fingers on the keyboard and avoided eye contact. "Almost as if you wanted to avoid the family."

Bear grunted and looked away. Geniuses were so annoying sometimes. Of course, he was avoiding the family. Well, not Rayray, of course. Twins before wins. But he couldn't face his stepfather's disapproval or Mom's concern.

"Staying for roast night?"

Bear cringed.

"I'll take that as a no." His 'lil bro had somehow perfected the art of dry retorts since he saw him last. "Is that everything you need?"

Bear frowned and studied Mike's tense mouth and crinkled brow. "Yeah, I guess. Unless you can think of anything else that will help with this job."

Mike swore under his breath.

What was his problem?

"If I come up with anything else," Mike said. "I'll send it to your phone, but for now I'll concentrate on what you've requested."

"Thanks, bro. You're the best," Bear said, and meant it. Mike had become very capable at what he did and would make an excellent computer engineer one day.

Or hacker. Or both.

"The breaker boxes will take time," Mike continued trying to fill the awkward silence with tech talk.

"How long?"

Mike shrugged. "A day or two? I have everything I need. I just have to make them."

Bear nodded. "Any luck on the owner or blueprints?"

Mike sighed, which in Mike's world meant, "sort of." Failure didn't exist in Mike's reality. Success was only a matter of time and equipment. "The owner is listed as S. Dow. The home address listed is for a West Vancouver convenience store."

"Fake address."

"Obviously." Mike turned to his computer and pulled up a window. He leaned back to let Bear look at the screen.

"What's this?"

"The official blueprint on file submitted to the city of Vancouver. I also sent the file to your email."

Bear took one glance at the schematic and scowled. "Fake as well."

Mike nodded and closed the window for the browser. "They didn't even bother trying to match the actual dimensions of the building or topography of the site. It's so lazy it's insulting."

Bear didn't need to ask how Mikey knew what the compound actually looked like. He would've found aerial shots online or failing that, he'd use the drone.

"So, no name, no address, and no building plans.

Why are you smiling like you just came out of a titty bar for the first time?"

Mike's grin widened and hit the enter key on his keyboard. Bear's phone pinged with a message. He pulled it out and tapped to access the text from Mike. The message contained a picture of a pretty woman, Asian descent, along with a name, address, and contact information. Mike even included a short bio of her professional affiliations and recent social media posts.

"Who's this?"

"The next best thing."

Chapter Six

"Never trust a computer nerd who doesn't have their own domain."

~ Michael Horowitz

Turned out the next best thing was the lead architect for the building project. Mike possessed the skills and knowledge to remote hack the architect's computer, pass the firewall and deluxe security software, but Bear couldn't ask that of his younger brother. It was one thing for Mike to supply Bear with materials so Bear could go off and break the law, it was another thing entirely to ask his 'lil bro to do it for him.

Apparently, there were still some lines Bear refused to cross.

So annoying.

Luckily, Mike wasn't the only Crawford with computer skills. Bear only needed to connect or hack into the same Wi-Fi connection as the architect and from there, infiltrate her records from within. Security software drove people to have a false sense of protection. In reality, their own actions left them vulnerable to anyone with the know-how and motivation.

Bear settled down at a small circular pedestal table and took out his laptop. He was fortunate to grab one of the last available seats with his back and computer facing the wall. He preferred not to break the law in front of witnesses wherever and whenever possible. Despite the "casual" atmosphere of cafés, these coffee and tea drinkers alike tended to be nosy—all in the name of "people watching."

An image of his twin's outrage at his judgemental thought made him smile. Ha!

Bear took a swig of his steaming hot latté and winced. His teeth ached. He'd have to wait for the drink to cool down a little.

Anne Cho sat down at the table across the aisle from him. Her gaze briefly met his and she flashed him a polite smile. Dressed for business in a pantsuit and flats, she'd styled her black hair into some sort of stylish knot. Juni, his youngest sister, would know what it was called, but Bear didn't care. Whatever the name, it suited her and left her face unencumbered. Her skin glowed and her eyes scanned the laptop's screen, while her hands flew across the keyboard.

His computer dinged. He turned off the sound and smiled. Ms. Cho connected to the café's Wi-Fi. Perfect.

The architect's phone buzzed, and she answered it without taking her gaze off the screen.

Bear's smile grew as he worked his way into her system. He took another swig of coffee. This would be a cakewalk.

"Yes, I saw it," Ms. Cho hissed into her phone. The warm and appreciative tone she'd used to order coffee had disappeared.

Bear paused and listened.

"Your idea of promoting women in construction is a picture of heels for the boardroom and boots for the jobsite with a lame slogan saying we can have it all."

She paused.

"I don't care if there was a designer purse and a hard helmet."

Bear winced for the person on the other end of the phone call. He'd stalked Ms. Cho's social media. She didn't hesitate to speak her mind.

Currently, she paused to listen to the person's response.

"How tone-deaf are you?" she asked.

Bear chuckled into his latté, only to flinch when Ms. Cho looked up and snapped her angry gaze on him.

He saluted her with his coffee cup and tried not to

outright laugh when she called him a douche under her breath.

He needed to focus on getting this job done while the architect sat at a long table, sipping her latté, and ripping into her co-worker. With a few clicks and taps of the keyboard, Bear accessed her personal and confidential documents. Ms. Cho should've known better than to connect to public Wi-Fi, but she also probably didn't expect someone to follow her for days waiting for the opportunity.

After five minutes of perusing the architect's files, Bear knew she was as organized as she was capable. Best news ever. Thieves loved obsessive compulsive, type-A targets. They made it easy to find things. Everything was logically labelled and ordered.

Since Bear already had the plot ID for the compound, he found the plans and downloaded them to his computer in minutes. He'd feel bad stealing from an innocent architect whose only crime was completing a job, but none of this would blow back to her.

He disconnected from the Wi-Fi and leaned back in his seat. Now he could finish his coffee and be one with the people watchers.

Ms. Cho hung up her call and glared at her phone before going back to work. Her gaze scanned the screen with hyper-focus again. Nothing about her posture or expression indicated she realized the breach in her computer security.

Bear finished his latté and packed up. So far, this job was going smoother than he expected. The building plan glitch was solved without too much delay or complications. Now, he needed to work on a plan to get through the compound undetected.

Bear rubbed his neck to smooth down the prickling sensation. He'd pulled off a lot of jobs without complications. Why did this one feel different? Why did this one send his gut into churning summersaults?

Bear scowled and left the café. Only time would give him the answers to those questions.

Chapter Seven

"Stealing is a lazy man's way. Something for nothing, leaves you hell to pay."

~ Michael Peterson

Bear scaled the stone wall and hopped onto the wide ledge at the top. The moonless night bathed him in muted light from far away stars, while the security lights swathed the complex below in stark brightness. Tasha landed close by and looked at him for orders. She'd already helped him gain entry to the inner perimeter by providing a nice distraction.

The late summer wind brushed by, ruffling black

hair in his face and teasing the collar of his worn leather jacket. He surveyed the layout of the facility below. If the owner of this compound was a simple merchant, Bear was a pink unicorn shifter. No low-level supplier from the Underworld had this many safeguards, and Bear would know. He stole from a number of them regularly.

This complex was different. He'd already slipped past numerous magical protections and rotating guards. Being half-fae provided few advantages in life, but this was one of those times not having much power was a benefit. His meager magic didn't trip the alarms as long as he wore his charmed ring and didn't use his magic near the wards.

Arrogant fae. They only associated power and competence with magic.

Bear lifted his head to the warm night and croaked. His magic had two sides to it. The passive side didn't require any conscious thought. Corvids were naturally drawn to him and wanted to please him. Given time, birds would surround him and bring him things they thought he wanted, like shiny pebbles and broken glass. The active side of his magic required intentional effort, drew from his corvid essence and allowed him to forcefully call the birds to him. He didn't need to wait if he wanted lots of corvids to swarm him. If he chose, he could also use his magic to compel the birds to do his bidding, whatever that may be.

The call wasn't pretty or delicate, but it was the call of the corvids and his one true talent in life. A human dog whistle, but for birds.

The energy of nearby crows and ravens pinged against his mind.

That's right, my pretties. Come to Daddy.

If only he shared his sister's talent. He would've completed the dangerous job already. He'd be resting on his stacks of money with his feet up drinking a cold one.

More unease crept along his spine, but he shook it off. All his jobs carried risk, and they all rang a few warning bells. This was no different.

Besides, the bigger the risk, the bigger the reward.

Ravens and crows swooped around him and perched on nearby tree limbs, the stone wall and ledges on the building. Less than he expected. That had been happening more and more lately. He wasn't sure if something was happening to the bird populations in the area or whether he was losing his touch.

He croaked again, singing a song only ravens and crows loved, but a song nonetheless. Weaving in corvid energy, he asked the birds to join him on an adventure.

Join me, he sang. *Make mischief with me. Mischief and mayhem.*

Though he could command them if he chose, he asked instead. The next steps would be dangerous, and he didn't want the birds unwittingly harmed.

More birds swooped in. Some hopped along the wall to get closer, naturally drawn to his power. They cocked their heads and blinked their beady black eyes while he asked them to come play with him.

Tasha's energy pulsed with excitement.

Of course, they were in. Of course, they'd join him. Corvids loved making a little mischief, just like cats were curious and dogs liked to sniff butts.

Bear swung his leg over the side of the wall and slid down to the complex grounds. His feet crunched dry grass. The post-collapse air funk cleared, indicating the owner had either paid fairies for an air filter spell or cast the spell himself. Probably the latter.

Well, that confirmed it. The client was full of shit. This guy wasn't a merchant. The two security walls, variety of magical detection spells and the air filter said so. A dark fae lord being shady wasn't exactly a surprise.

Fae couldn't be trusted.

He didn't normally work for the fae due to their deceptiveness and strong magic, and if he survived this job, he would make it a personal rule never to do so again. He would've said no to this job, but that choice had been taken from him the moment the client showed him that picture. No wasn't an option, and neither was failure.

Even success carried a risk.

Bear had finally taken one bad job too many and he only had himself to blame.

The birds moved ahead and played in front of the security cameras while he crouched down by the fence with wire cutters. He cut the wires, pulled the fencing to the side and scrambled through. A murder of crows branched off from the rest and moved to the next camera. The birds cackled and cawed in the air, flying and playing with delight. He envied their freedom and another pang of jealousy for his sister's powers stabbed his heart.

A large raven swooped down and landed on his shoulder. He winced. The bird's talons dug into the sensitive skin around his shoulder muscles. This bird wasn't Tasha. Was he the same one who'd joined him on the park bench weeks ago? The same one who attacked that backstabbing client months ago? Did Tasha have competition for his affections?

I'm Hugie, the bird croaked in his mind. *I'll be your general.*

Bear winced again. The motherfucker was loud. And surprisingly coherent. The birds didn't often speak to him, not even Tasha.

We are robbing Shadow Man? Hugie asked.

Yes. Is that a problem?

No. We like Shadow Man, but we like you more.

Bear waited for the birds to finish getting in place. A few had flown ahead to look for guards. The rest would continue to perch or play in front of the security cameras as he made his way through the compound.

Why do you rob Shadow Man? Hugie asked. *He's dangerous.*

Well, wasn't that a pleasant thought? No matter how dangerous this Shadow Man was, though, the dark fae lord who "offered" him this job scared Bear more.

The bird waited for his response.

Bear needed to be careful here. Ravens and crows

automatically wanted to please him and loved to create a little mischief, but they weren't inherently bad creatures. They were attentive and affectionate.

I'm making mischief, he answered.

The bird ruffled his feathers and settled his wings back. He studied Bear with his beady eyes and cocked his head. The bird didn't believe him.

Bear might not read minds, but the body language told its own truths. *If I don't, I die,* he told the raven.

We'll make sure Shadow Man not hurt you.

He sighed in relief. Even one defector could send the whole group of birds off into the night. *Thanks, bud.*

He turned his attention back to the compound as he approached the outer wall of the outermost building in a crouched position. A conspiracy of ravens moved with him as he picked his way through the compound. Thankfully, he'd memorized the schematics from the architect's plans.

The Shadow Man had a large windowless room in the center of the central building with walls five times as thick as any of the other walls. The vault had to be there. Bear turned in that direction and kept moving.

Hugie launched from his shoulders and disappeared into the night with heavy wingbeats while Bear kept his step light on the paved walkway. His sneakers still managed to scuff the ground and the flap of wings overhead punctured the silent night.

No alarms so far. At least not the kind he could hear.

He crept along the path until the central building came into view. A crow's cry was the only warning he got. He dove to the ground, tucked his chin and rolled. Something powerful struck the wall of the building beside him. Brick and mortar exploded, the debris catching his cheek before he turned away. Heart punching his chest, Bear sprang to his feet and ran for cover.

Footsteps echoed down the walkway.

On left, Hugie squawked in his mind.

Bear ducked in time to miss a fist flying at his face. He stepped to the side and drove his left fist into the face of the masked guard. The man crumpled to the ground, smacking the pavement. Bear crouched down, grabbed the guard's gun and stuffed it in the waistband of his jeans.

Incoming, Hugie croaked.

Bear sidestepped another attack. This masked guard blocked his counterpunch and kicked out to sweep Bear off his feet. Bear stepped over the kick, grabbed the man's extended arm and hooked the ankle of the kicking leg with his own. He twisted and brought down his weight on the man's bent leg. A sickening crunch and wail sent the birds aloft from their perches. The guard groaned and Bear slipped his arm under his neck while moving behind him.

Bear mentally pushed the birds back to their positions. Had he been exposed? Had anyone in the guard room seen? Heard the scream? Was one of these guards the shooter or was there someone else? Had they raised an alarm?

Locking his arms and hands in a classic figure four head lock, he applied pressure to the back of the man's neck and head. The man thrashed. Bear's breath became irregular and his heart raced. He was breathing too fast. He had to calm down. A few seconds later, the guard went limp in the hold. Bear lowered him to the ground. Sweat trickled down his face.

Good, Hugie croaked. *No more guards. The rest are all on the outer wall. Just watch the cameras.*

Bear relaxed a little. He'd already bypassed the outer guards and defences without having to engage in combat. Though he could handle himself, especially when he embraced his corvid magic and got advanced notice from his little buds, he wasn't invincible. And he wasn't a killer.

No racing footsteps echoed down the corridors. Hugie was right. No more guards. He straightened and closed the distance to the door with the security panel.

He considered the door lock. High tech. Expensive. And not infallible.

Nothing was these days. Not when Bear had a little bro who excelled in everything tech, including bypass keys and breaker boxes for all the common manufacturers of security control panels. He pulled out his toolkit and selected the small screwdriver to remove the cover of the panel. He carefully extracted the front of the panel with the screen to expose the motherboard inside. Noting the company name and model number, Bear dug into his toolkit again, this time extracting the matching code breaker box.

Thank you, Mike.

Bear plucked wires out of the toolkit and applied one end of a connector to the panel's small motherboard and the other end to the code breaker box. He repeated the action for two more wires. He hated this part of the job. No matter how many times Bear practiced or worked on his fine motor skills, connecting these stupid small pinchers to the right locations on the stupid small motherboard pissed him off. As Mike often told him, his large hands might be great at breaking stuff, like faces, but he was crap at the finer details. The gloves didn't help either.

The red light on the breaker box lit up, indicating it successfully drew from a power source. The small motor hummed in his hand and Mike's breaker box worked its own kind of magic.

Oooo shiny. Hugie landed on a nearby ledge and leaned in to watch. Corvids were curious by nature but this one was different than the others who'd flocked to the area to help him out. He'd even managed to scare Tasha off. Why?

The lights on the panel's screen flashed green and the door lock clicked open. Bear shook his head and shoved the thoughts of mysterious birds to the back of his mind. He straightened from his crouch, grabbed the door handle with his gloved hand and turned. The large metal security door popped open. The tension knotting his shoulders eased.

You're good at mischief making, Hugie croaked in

his mind and launched into the air.

Bear held the door open as he disconnected the breaker box and stuffed his supplies in his toolkit.

Your father would be proud...

Bear whipped around and looked for Hugie. The large bird had already disappeared in the night, but his words still echoed in Bear's mind.

What the fuck? Terry would only be disappointed to learn how low his son stooped. Bear's hold on the door slipped. He flung his other hand out before the door clicked shut. The metal door slammed against his fingers and pain raced up his arm. Bear winced. *Motherfucker.*

He thanked the other birds and told them to leave after he shut the door. Tasha shot him images of flying in the night sky once again, wanting him to join her. He wished he could. But Bear wouldn't be flying out of here. He wouldn't be exiting the same way he entered, either. Pulling the door open, he shook his hand like it would somehow relieve the throbbing pain and slipped inside the building. A tingle of air immediately passed over him. Magic.

In a breath, he drew in his laughable essence as the magical screen washed over him. The ring charm only worked if he wasn't actively using his power. The tingling sensation faded, and he continued to breathe. No death magic invaded his soul. He grunted and moved forward, stopping multiple times as more magical sensors screened him. The spell couldn't be triggered for life in general; otherwise, a fly or mouse or any living creature would trip the alarm, but surely this man with his money and magic could've found a way to set the wards to sense a human. But the Shadow Man simply hadn't bothered.

The arrogance of these dark fae was astounding. The idea of a reg, a non-Other from the Mortal Realm, infiltrating a secure compound and breaching the inner defences without magic was so inconceivable, the fae's last line of defense for his most prized possessions focused on magical presence instead of life.

Motion activated lights flickered on and Bear walked down the hall to another security door. His footsteps echoed in the cold empty space and a chill raced up his spine. No guards in here. The dark fae didn't trust anyone to get this close to his vault.

Bear needed to finish the job and get out.

The second security door, though made by a different manufacturer, proved no more difficult for one of Mike's breaker boxes to bypass than the first. He mouthed a silent thank you to Mike and ignored the stab of guilt.

He stepped into the vault and sucked in a breath. There, in the center of the room, suspended above a white podium by invisible threads of magic, hung the oddest black jewel he'd laid eyes on. Instead of reflecting the light, the gem absorbed it. Yet, despite its lack-lustre sparkle, something about it called to him. His sister Raven would love it. He wouldn't have been able to drag her from the room.

Bear shook his head. No. He wasn't here for pretty

baubles. Taking more than the item he sought might set off unseen alarms. Greed got thieves caught. He studied the room and found the item he'd been tasked to retrieve. Nestled in the corner of the room on a dusty shelf sat an intricate wooden box about the size of a softball with runes etched into each side like a die.

Bear strode over to the object and dug out his lodestone from the inside pocket of his jacket. The magical disc would transport him to a predetermined location and had cost him a small fortune to procure from the snobby fairies. Thankfully, it was reusable and well worth the cost. The dark fae lord had been very clear about what to do once he touched the Claíomh Solais. First, he needed to get out of the room as fast as possible as contact most likely would trip another alarm. Second, he needed to draw the runes the dark fae provided to prevent anyone from following him. And third, above all else, he wasn't to open the box.

With the exception of its pretty decorations, the box looked mundane, boring even, giving off no magical signature or anything special to indicate the hefty reward he'd receive for retrieving it. For all Bear knew, it could be a random hunk of wood two fae lords decided to steal back and forth to bide the time and ease their boredom. He doubted that. The gleam in the lord's eyes had been too fevered for this to be some twisted game of tag.

Bear took a deep breath and keyed the lodestone. A portal opened to the living room of his safe house. Now or never. He rubbed his hands together, ignored his racing heart, reached forward and gripped the decorated wooden box with both hands.

The moment his skin made contact, magic swept the room. The lights dimmed and wind from an unknown source jostled the air. Dark, potent fae energy pulsed and shook the vault. The wind picked up, creating a vortex of shadows and dust a few feet away.

Oh, fuck no.

Bear wrenched the box from the shelf and stepped through the portal. Before it closed, a man stepped out of the vortex created by wind, dust and shadows. Power rolled off him in thick, menacing waves. An imposing dark fae lord wearing full court armour with a black cape swirling in the portal wind behind him. Piercing black eyes of the Underworld met Bear's and the man's face contorted with rage.

Silver flashed.

Bear froze as a dagger aimed at his heart flew through the air. He hadn't seen the man throw it. He clutched the box to his chest and flinched.

The portal snapped shut.

Bear opened his eyes to find the living room of his safe house. No dagger. No blood. No dark fucking fae lord.

That was close. Too close.

He sank to his knees, still clutching the box and sucked in long drags of air. He couldn't stay like this. He could panic over the close call later. His client's warning voice nagged him. He lurched to his feet, placed the box on his coffee table, dug out a black marker from his pocket and hastily drew the runes on the wall. He had no wish to meet that Shadow Man ever again.

With his heart still caught in his throat, he scribbled the runes over and over again from memory and practice, until his hand ached. The entire time, the box sat on the coffee table, inert and unmoving, but he couldn't shake the feeling he was being watched.

Chapter Eight

"There's a little bit of magic in every box!"

~ Adam Rex

B ear stared at the wooden box and contemplated his sanity. His client had warned him repeatedly not to open it, like it would release devastation and destruction into the Mortal Realm. The longer he sat in its company, though, the more he believed that was another lie. The Claíomh Solais wasn't some Pandora's Box. This was something his client didn't want him to see. Why? Was he afraid Bear would take it for his own? Was it something too dangerous to release to another fae and the client worried Bear's morals would kick in and prevent him from handing it over?

Bear had taken his jacket off, cleaned up the cuts on his face from the ricochet and scuffles with the guards and found some ice for his hand. The rotating fan propped on the kitchen counter oscillated back and forth, bathing his back in recycled air every half a minute.

Poor Kissa. He'd left his spare key with a neighbour to go over and feed his cat if he didn't return in few days. He'd left Kissa yesterday afternoon and had only been gone the night, but if he didn't make it back by the end of today, he'd find little surprises in his shoes for the next week or two.

He loved that cat.

The lights above flickered as someone stomped in the room above his own. His attention drew back to the box. He hadn't told the dark fae lord when he planned to nab the Claíomh Solais, so he had a bit of time before he needed to make contact.

Time for what? He finished the job. Now it was time to collect the final payment. If that's what the client intended to give him. The more he sat and stared at the box, the more he suspected the client never intended to pay him. If he couldn't afford to let Bear glimpse what was inside the box, could he afford to let Bear live with the knowledge of who'd hired him to steal it?

Fuck. He'd really done it this time. He thought he'd

found a way to dig himself out of the criminal element, to turn to more legal avenues of generating income, and instead, he'd signed his death warrant.

He did have a contingency plan. Death instead of payment was always a possibility with the clientele he served. He reached into his pocket and ran his thumb along the cold surface of the lodestone. Would his flight or fight response be enough this time?

And how would he leave this apartment and the safety it provided by the runes with the Claíomh Solais without getting attacked by that other fae lord? If he met the client here, he'd have nowhere to run.

The fridge's annoying whirr faded as the runes on the strange wooden box drew him in again. The prickling sensation of being watched hadn't gone away, but the scary Shadow Man from the vault hadn't appeared to smite him, so the protective blocking runes must be working.

Claíomh Solais.

The White Glaive of Light.

He never would've picked this out of the room if his client hadn't provided a picture.

Don't open it, the dark fae lord had warned. *It will be your death.*

This entire time Bear assumed what was inside the box would kill him, but the more he thought about it, the more he realized it was his client who would kill him if he looked inside. And the client would also probably kill him for handing over the box unopened like a good little boy.

The knot in Bear's stomach told him what his brain still tried to catch up with—no matter what path he chose, death would greet him at the end.

Well, now. Wasn't that the truth for everything in life? He'd had a good run. Sort of. His shoulders slumped. No. There was so much more he wanted to do. So much more he wanted to be. He wished he'd been a better son and brother. He wished he'd gone back to the family.

He wasn't a complete failure. There were a few things to be proud of. He'd scrambled and found a way to make it on his own. He got the job done and paid his bills. He would've helped pay his sister's loans, too, if that stubborn mule would let him.

His gaze drifted back to the box again.

The Claíomh Solais.

He ran his finger along the engraved surface of the box again. He didn't get zapped. He had no premonitions or pain on contact. It was inert wood. He'd been sitting in his apartment for hours, alone, stroking wood.

His siblings would have a field day with that.

Ah, fuck it. If he was going to die no matter what, he wanted to know what was in the box. Sure, curiosity killed the cat, but at least the pussy got some answers.

Bear snatched the cube from the table and lifted it to his face to examine the runes closer. No seam for a lid. No keyhole. No spell to recite. He already knew rubbing it like a lamp didn't produce a genie.

The Claíomh Solais couldn't be opened by physical

means. That left the other kind. Bear groaned. Why did it have to be magic? He set the box down again and reached inside himself. He probably didn't have enough magic to open it. Pulling his corvid essence out, he wound his power around the cube.

The wooden box with the intricate engravings began to hum.

Bear pulled more magic and wrapped it in another layer. He'd never done anything like this before. Since he couldn't use his powers to shift into an animal, he assumed all he could do with this stuff was call birds to him. Of course, he'd tried all sorts of things when he was younger, but he gave up after nothing found success. This, though. Something about this curious little wooden box with the engravings...Something called to him like he called to his birds.

The box hummed louder, a delicate, bell-like sound tinkled from inside.

He pulled more power, more power than he'd ever pulled before, more power than he thought he had and swathed the Claíomh Solais in his magic. The box burst open. Magic rushed out and flung Bear back in his seat. Pure light streamed out. Bear shielded his eyes from the intense glow and ducked down as the blinding light chased away all the shadows in his small apartment. Heat pressed against his skin and his heart beat furiously.

Something thumped on the floor and tumbled along the carpet to rest on his foot. He looked down to find the box laying benign and empty on the carpet.

The lighting in the room dimmed and the room cooled down. Bear lowered his arm. In front of him, in a glow of dazzling light, like a phoenix rising from its ashes, a woman dressed in ordinary jeans and a tank top stood with her hands on her hips and her feet shoulder width apart. The light highlighted her high cheekbones, smooth dark skin and shining platinum hair. Black eyes of the Underworld, eyes like his, studied him and her full red lips curled up with amusement. She was by far the most beautiful woman he'd ever seen.

His twin sister, Raven, had once told him his exterior was far prettier than who he was inside. She didn't normally talk to him like that, but she'd been especially pissed off at him for something. He couldn't remember what he'd done that particular time, but he deserved it. He always did. And despite her words being spoken in anger, she wasn't wrong.

Bear never lacked female attention. Women enjoyed his company and he enjoyed theirs. He put minimal, if any, effort into seducing a woman. He didn't need to. That wasn't arrogance, but experience. He never had to work for anything. He certainly didn't have to beg.

One mere second in this woman's company, and he wanted to crawl on the floor and grovel before her.

And that was all kinds of wrong.

Bjorn motherfucking Crawford did not beg.

"Who...who the fuck are you?" He pointed at her. "And get off my coffee table."

The woman laughed, a tinkling bell-like sound that made him think of fairies and pixie dust and fields full of flowers. She smelled like a bouquet of wild roses.

"My name is Chloe." Her melodious voice lilted with an Underworld accent and sent a jolt straight to his dick.

Nope. Not happening.

She stepped from the coffee table and set her unflinching gaze on him once again. "But the more interesting question is who are you?"

"It doesn't matter who I am." And it really didn't. He needed to know what she did with the Claíomh Solais. He couldn't exactly shove her back in the box and hand her over. Even if he knew how, the dark fae lord would definitely hunt him down and kill him for the deception. He glanced at the container and picked it up. "What did you do with it?"

"With what?"

"The Claíomh Solais."

Her full lips split into a wide grin revealing teeth as white as her hair. "Do you not know?"

He balled his hands into fists. "No."

"I *am* the Claíomh Solais."

Chapter Nine

"Surprise is key in all art."

~ *Oscar Niemeyer*

B ear stared at the striking woman in front of him and the same thought repeated over and over in his head: What. The. Fuck?

He'd wonder why the dark fae lord left out this one crucial detail, but he already knew the answer. He wasn't supposed to open the box. The client never intended for him to find out he'd stolen an actual person.

What the fuck?

Again and again, the thought repeated as anger rose from within and heated his blood. Bear had stooped to some pretty low lows—breaking laws where necessary, cracking some skulls, lying, stealing—but never this low. There were some lines he refused to cross.

Chloe studied the room, focusing on his hastily drawn runes along the walls. She dropped her head back and laughed—a raucous roar of bells. She clutched her stomach and laughed some more.

He folded his arms in front of his chest and waited. Her Underworld power continued to flow from her skin, beckoning him to come closer and play in the waves. From the second she burst from the box, he'd had to lock his knees to physically prevent himself from being drawn in by her power.

She flung out an arm and pointed at the nearest rune. "Do you know what these are?"

He shifted his weight on his feet, not sure if he'd need to subdue her, fight her or run. "They trap the essence of the Claíomh Solais and prevent anyone from forming a portal to the 'object.'"

She laughed some more and shook her head. Her platinum hair brushed against her face as her shoulders shook. "Oh, you're not wrong about that. But whomever gave these to you to use didn't tell you how they worked, did they?" She glanced around the sparse apartment and then at him, her gaze appraising while still managing to dance with amusement. "You're a thief. You weren't meant to open the box with the runes drawn."

This was apparently hilarious to Chloe and set her off on another fit of laughter. "I'm sorry. That was rude of me." She wiped a tear from her eye.

"What kind of monster locks a person in a box?" Bear asked. The memory of the Shadow Man emerging from darkness with rage contorting his face into a death mask surged up. He'd moved so fast, Bear hadn't seen the dagger before the weapon flew through the air perfectly aimed at his heart. Bear's death had awaited him in that vault. And it still waited for him. Returning the box wasn't an option.

Bear shivered. The Shadow Man locked this woman in a box. Why? Dark fae were deceptive and rarely what they seemed. Was the Shadow Man as vicious and as lethal as he looked, or was Chloe not as sweet as she appeared?

Bear leaned closer as if to examine her. "Or are you some monster that needs to be caged?"

Chloe cocked her head. "Dark fae live a long time. I grew weary and wanted to disconnect from the politics and squabbling for a few years. You and your alluring magic woke me up."

Bear straightened without even meaning to. She found him alluring?

Gah! No, Bear. No. Do not fall for the fae. Do not be fooled by her considerable charms.

Odin-loving dark fae and their seductive ways. He wouldn't fall for this nonsense. Bear snarled. "Stop it."

"Stop what?"

"Trying to seduce me with your magic." He waved

a hand in the air as if to clear a thick cloud of perfume.

"Oh, that's not me."

Cryptic, too. Seductive and cryptic.

"What are you going to do?" She changed the subject and batted her long lashes at him. "Are you going to give this defenceless woman to your master?"

"Client."

She smirked.

"And no. I draw the line at human trafficking."

"Oooo." She straightened. "A thief with morals. How very Robin Hood." Her gaze sparkled. She mocked him. Minx.

"I'll give him the box."

"No, you won't."

"Why not? We'll close it up and hand it over." He'd still have to run for his life, but he didn't see any other option. Maybe he could make a deal with the other dark fae—the one who tried to kill him. Sure. Sounded like a great plan.

She shook her head, her white hair whispering against her shoulders. "He'll kill you on the spot. You won't have time to run. He'll know the moment he sees the box that I'm no longer inside. It would be better to run now."

"You almost sound worried for me."

"I'm growing strangely attached to you, Pretty Boy. It would be a shame to waste that face."

He scowled and she responded by laughing like a fucking fairy.

Chapter Ten

"Don't worry, it only seems kinky the first time."

~ Unknown

Bear nursed his beer and glared at his new guest from across the small dining table. She perched on a matching chair acting as if she wasn't sending off some serious dark fae sex vibes.

"That's not nice, you know," she said, her angelic voice breaking the heavy silence between them.

He tensed his muscles to prevent himself from leaping over the table to touch her. This was ridiculous. She was the one who should stop. "What's not nice?"

"Glaring. It's rude. You stole me, not the other way around. I'm not sure what you're so pissed about."

"I'm pissed that you keep trying to use your magic on me. That's what's *not nice*."

She dropped her hands away from her water and laughed. The sound sent blood rushing to his dick. Yup. Ri-dick-ulous. He ground his teeth together and growled. When she didn't stop chuckling, he drank more of his beer.

"Is this how you deal with women you're attracted to?"

Bear choked on his drink. "Attra...what? That's—"

She waved his protest away. "You must have an awful love life."

"My love life is just fine, thank you," he sputtered. The memory of Janice's last phone call flared like a bad case of indigestion. He flinched. Whatever. Chloe had no way of knowing about that.

"Sure...sure..." Her lips twitched.

He wanted nothing more than to smash his mouth against hers and feel that wicked tongue on his skin. He squeezed his eyes shut for a second instead. "Unbelievable."

Her eyebrows shot up, mocking him with feigned innocence. "If this attraction is so unsettling to you, we could always act on it and cut the tension." She leaned forward, mouth slightly parted, black irises bleeding out to cover the whites of her eyes. "It would be an enjoyable way to pass the time while you figure out what you're going to do."

Bear slammed his bottle down on the table.

Chloe giggled and brushed her white hair back from her smooth skin.

He jabbed his finger in the air at her. "You will stop this act and I will make a plan."

She flopped back in her chair. The cheap wood creaked. "I'm not actively doing a thing."

He glared.

"But fine. Let's make a deal." She placed on hand over her heart. "I won't try to improve your love life."

He snapped his mouth shut.

"And you will feed me. And soon or all bets are off. I'm not responsible for my actions when I'm hungry."

"I'm starting to realize why someone locked you in a magical block of wood."

She laughed again and his traitorous body pulsed in response.

Bear watched Chloe inhale the pizza at an alarming rate. It was one of those fancy kinds of pizza, not the regular pepperoni and cheese he normally ordered. The look on her face when he read out the description for this gourmet option made him cave. Who was he to deny a pretty lady who'd been stuck in a magical box for who-knew-how-long good pizza? It's not as though it had pickles on it. That would be an abomination to the world of pizza and it had no place in his home.

The smell of greasy dough, cheese, chorizo sausage

and a whole slew of veggies and herbs he couldn't name filled the room. But it wasn't the pizza that made his mouth water.

Chloe licked her fingers and met his gaze. She took her time sucking the grease off the last finger.

He dropped his slice of pizza. It flopped onto his plate with a cheesy splat.

"Stop it," he hissed, not shaking the feeling of déjà vu.

"I'm sorry. I can't help it. You're so easy to...excite." She smirked and reached for her glass of water. After taking a long sip, she set it down and met his gaze. "Do you honestly have no idea why you feel the way you do?"

"Oh, I know."

She pulled another slice of pizza from the box. "Enlighten me then,"

He waved his hand at her. "You're obviously weaving some sort of dark fae spell on me. I'd have to be a corpse not to respond to the magic coupled with your beauty."

Her irises bled out again and he squashed the urge to go to her.

She blinked and rested her half-eaten pizza slice on the plate. "I take it you don't have a lot of experience with dark fae."

Bear bristled. He was experienced where he needed to be, thank you very much.

Chloe ignored his reaction and continued. "The fae magic that radiates off me is unintentional. It drifts from me just as it does with you. You're more sensitive to my power because you find me attractive and our magic is compatible. That's all."

Bear snatched his beer from the table and took a long drink. "Are you going to dish some fated mate bullshit?"

Chloe laughed again, the sound addictive. A thought smacked Bear in the face. He'd do anything in his power to see her dazzling smile and hear that enchanting laugh again. Anything.

He drank more beer. What the fuck? He didn't care what she said. Fae couldn't be trusted and this shit wasn't natural. She'd woven a powerful spell over him. That had to be it.

"Fated mates?" Chloe's tone was amused. "No. Absolutely not. Have you been reading your sister's romance novels again?"

"Again?" How'd she know he had a sister?

She smiled as if she knew some deep secret of his.

"I only read one section one time to see what all the fuss was about." Raven had practically shoved the book in his hands and told him if he wanted to actually be a "decent fucking human being" he'd read it as if it was a manual to a woman's heart. Weirdo. Like she was some love expert.

She crossed her arms and smirked again. "And?"

"And it was unrealistic. No man could possibly live up to the expectations set by Joe Roth. Nobody can read minds like that. It only sets women up for disappointment."

Chloe's smirk spread into a wide smile. "Struck a nerve, did I?"

He shut his mouth again. Anything he said now would come across as defensive. He had no reason to feel that way.

"Have you never spoken with a fae before? Has no one shown you the root of your power?"

He looked away and squeezed his beer bottle a little too tightly. "My mother strictly forbade us to go into the Underworld and I never had any opportunities for a long heart to heart with a random fae about my inadequacies."

Chloe cocked her head.

"What?"

She shrugged. "You don't seem like the type to listen to orders or rules when they're in the way of something you want. You could've defied your mother."

"You have obviously never met Elizabeth Crawford."

Chloe laughed. "So, you haven't met any dark fae? At all?"

"I've met some."

"Women?"

He narrowed his eyes, not sure what she was getting at.

"I'm assuming you're a heterosexual male fae who's only met other male fae so there was no attraction involved." She paused to wink. "At least not from your end of things."

He opened his mouth to protest and she held up her hand to stop him. "Surely, you've met women before where you were instantly attracted to them."

"Sure."

"That's what this is, only our compatible magic emphasizes it."

"Emphasizes?" More Underworld dark fae bullshit.

"Accentuates, highlights, stresses...Yeah. Emphasizes. It might be potent and intoxicating, but you have free will. You don't have to act on it." She leaned over her plate with the forgotten slice. "But it's more fun if you do."

"What makes our magic compatible?" He gulped down the rest of his beer, trying not to show her how important her answer was. How could anything be a match to his puny power? Unless it was a yin and yang sort of thing. Her bold, impressive magic of mammoth proportions to his rinky-dink, dawdling power.

Bear swallowed the bitter beer and waited for Chloe to finish studying him like a lab rat.

"You really have no clue, do you?"

"And you do?"

She nodded.

"Enlighten me, then," he said, using her own words from earlier.

She smiled and leaned back in her chair again, the soft lighting making her skin glow, warm and inviting.

"My power is all about shining light on darkness."

"Darkness?"

She shrugged. "Literal or figurative. Secrets, lies,

hidden truths." She skewered him with an imperceptible gaze. "Self-made barriers."

Bear frowned. "Barriers? I don't have any of those. Surely, I would remember constructing magical walls."

Chloe cocked her head at him. "Haven't you? I can sense it. A giant barricade with a wealth of magic behind it, leaking out of cracks and crevices. One day, your dam will break, and it will be magnificent."

Bear snorted. "Were you imprisoned because of hallucinations, by any chance?"

"I'm quite serious."

"So am I."

Chloe frowned and pursed her lips. "Did you experience any trauma when you were younger?"

"Describe trauma?"

"A moment of great pain or sadness, physical or mental."

Bear sat back and a memory crashed into his mind— a memory full of sadness and pain. The first time Raven shifted with Mom and Dad—Terry—and Bear didn't. He couldn't. It was in that moment, Bear realized he would never be able to join them. Not like that. He would always be different and apart from his shifter family. He could call birds to him, but he'd never transform. He'd never join them. He'd never be like them. He'd never be one of them. And he wanted so desperately to belong.

Chloe's knowing gaze burned. He looked away, wanting to say something scathing or mean. Lash out. Maybe tell her to fuck off.

But he couldn't do that. He couldn't speak to her like that.

It would be so easy to lie and tell her she knew nothing. But he couldn't do that, either. Because she did. She saw through everything, even the cloaking ring, and she scared the shit out of him.

Chapter Eleven

"Fuck it."

~ *Bear's final thought before making decisions*

Bear glanced over his shoulder for the third time since leaving Chloe behind in his rune-protected apartment. The dark fae lord had assured him as long as the runes were drawn, they'd trap the Claíomh Solais and prevent anyone from portalling into the apartment. But the client had also banked on Bear not opening the box.

Bear waited in the apartment building's hallway for almost an hour to see if she'd emerge.

Nothing.

She didn't even try the door handle. When she found out today's date, she'd wanted to watch television and "catch up." Exactly how long had she been trapped in that box? She wouldn't say.

Tasha clicked as she flew overhead, occasionally stopping on awnings, windowsills or ledges to click at him some more. He didn't need to speak bird to know she was both telling him off for the disappearing act at the same time as expressing her excitement to see him again.

A man walking in the opposite direction on the sidewalk rammed his shoulder into Bear's.

"Hey! Watch it, asshole!" the man barked over his shoulder.

Bear waved at him with his middle finger and kept walking. If he ran into someone, he'd normally apologize, but the other man had been walking side by side with his buddy and the two of them had taken over more than half the sidewalk. Why should Bear have to flatten himself against the wall to let two inconsiderate strangers walk past?

"Didn't you hear me, asshole?" A large, heavy hand clamped on Bear's shoulder and tugged.

Bear spun with the motion and blocked the predictable punch to the face with his arm. He stepped inside the man's guard, grabbed both his shoulders and whipped his head forward.

Crack!

The man reeled back from the head butt and

clutched his spurting nose. "Phuuck."

Bear ignored him and turned to his buddy. "You want to come at me, too?"

The friend shook his head, raised his hands and backed away.

Everyone stared. Great. Low profile blown. His heart pumped blood hard enough the pounding of it drowned out all other sounds. He rounded his shoulders, turned back and ducked around the next corner. He didn't want to make a scene and here he was getting into scraps on the sidewalk on the East Side. Stupid.

Not wanting to risk the main streets, he made his way through the filthy side streets to the local convenience store that sold everything from onions to cell phone cases decorated with kitties. He needed a burner phone, and in less than twenty minutes, he walked out of the store with one set up.

When the next SkyTrain slid to a squeaky halt, he hopped on and ignored Tasha's indignant squawk. She'd find him again soon enough. She always did.

Bear got his lodestone ready and pulled out the business card of the dark fae. He stared at his phone. Maybe he should call Raven. Not for advice or help—he didn't want his twin mixed up in this—but just to hear her voice. He knew his distance hurt her. He hurt his whole family, including himself. But he just couldn't...

He gripped the phone and looked away. Swallowing a lump in his throat, he shook his head as if it would magically clear his thoughts.

He couldn't bring himself to admit he'd been wrong. So wrong.

Bear had planned to make it big and roll back into the family house a successful man, proving to Terry he could make it on his own, doing things his own way. Instead, he was a thief and broke every single code of ethics Terry tried to instill in him.

He glanced at the card. Well, almost every code. There was still some honour left in him after all. Bear might've finally taken one bad job too many, but at least he'd dictate how things ended. On his terms.

He should've paid more attention to the early warning signs and turned down this job before meeting with the dark fae lord and crossing that point of no return. If he hadn't taken the job, though, someone else would have. Chloe would still be in the box and the Claíomh Solais would end up in someone else's hands. Literally.

Anger bubbled up inside him, and he turned the phone on. While he punched in the number, he took another deep breath.

The dark fae lord picked up on the first ring, his deep voice rattling the phone's cheap speakers. "Is it done?"

Bear had been unsure of what to say or do, but the hard, detached voice of the dark fae lord confirmed Bear's belief he couldn't under any circumstances hand Chloe over to him, nor would lying get him far. Even if this choice meant his death, he had to stand for something. Maybe one day his family would be proud of him, proud that he finally made the right choice and protected something other than himself.

He closed his eyes.

All this time he searched for a way to prove himself without having the ability to shift, and the answer had been there the whole time. Raven was right. He was an idiot.

"You didn't tell me the Claíomh Solais was a woman," Bear growled. He briefly considered denying any knowledge of Chloe and lying about completing the job, but the dark fae lord would find out. Spies abounded in the Underworld and at least one fae already knew of the theft. Shadow Man.

Silence met his statement.

"The deal is fucking off. Women aren't property or chattel."

A couple of passengers blanched and stared at him with round eyes. He turned away from them to look out the window as metro Vancouver whizzed by.

"You weren't supposed to open the box." The dark fae lord's voice dropped dangerously low.

"I'm dead either way." The cars on the SkyTrain jostled a little as they rounded a corner.

The silence meeting Bear's analysis confirmed he was right. At least this man didn't insult him with lies. Instead, after another long pause, he said, "Bring Chloe to me."

"Go fuck yourself." Bear hung up. He did the right thing, but a sense of dread settled over him and clamped onto his gut. He'd stolen from one dangerous dark fae lord and he'd backed out of a deal with another. It was only a matter of time before one or both caught up with him.

Maybe he could make a deal with the fae he stole Chloe from. His memory flashed to the fae's deadly expression and the flash of metal. Yeah, sure. Make a deal with a man who threw a knife at his chest. He'd already contemplated that idea and it was just as dumb as the first time the thought crossed his mind. He wouldn't get past showing his face. That fae was definitely the type who killed first and asked questions later.

Bear swallowed and pulled his shoulders back. He'd find a solution to this problem. He always did. Like the corvids he commanded, he was resourceful. And when he figured out a safe way to return, he'd go to his family and make things right.

Bear dismantled the phone and chucked it in the garbage at the next stop before hopping on the next train. He had the rest of the Millennium Line loop to figure out what to do before heading back to the safe house.

To Chloe.

Chapter Twelve

"I think my soulmate might be carbs."
~ Unknown, but also Bear's sister, Raven

Bear pushed open the apartment door and slipped inside. The cool air brushed his face and chased away some of the heat from the late summer's day.

Chloe sat at the kitchen counter and sipped water from one of the two glasses he had in the cupboard. Unexpected relief washed through him. She was still here.

An open window let a gentle breeze into the

apartment, and confirmed it didn't matter if the doors and windows were opened, closed, or locked, the runes trapped Chloe inside.

"What?" Chloe set her glass down. "No menacing dark fae lord trailing behind you to whisk me away?"

Bear shut the door with his foot and turned the deadbolt. "No. I told you I wasn't a human trafficker and I meant it."

"Some would argue I shouldn't get the same consideration as a human."

Anger flared. Who were these people? An overwhelming urge to hunt them down and beat them rose up from within. Bear pushed the feelings down, took a deep breath and unclenched his free hand. He'd struggled to control his emotions since he "met" Chloe.

Bear paused.

Okay, he'd always had a temper, but over the years he'd developed coping mechanisms that allowed him to have a better handle on it. Chloe's presence in his life definitely derailed his self-control.

He needed to go back and find the jerk from the sidewalk and get rid of some of this rage. Smashing someone's face always worked as a backup coping strategy. If he kept this anger bottled up much longer, it would burn a hole through his side.

Chloe looked down into the glass of water. "And so many say one thing and then do another." Pain briefly flashed across her face.

Forget finding that guy and fighting. He wanted to erase that look, chase it away. He stepped forward, then stopped. What would he do? Say? What would make things better?

Her pain was gone before he took his next breath. His shoulders sagged and a realization smacked him in the brain. She didn't need him to get rid of the bad stuff, she did it on her own. She didn't need him for anything.

Instead of rushing to her, he held up the shopping bag and shook the contents.

"Doing your part to contribute to the global plastic crisis?" She lifted a dark eyebrow.

"I got some supplies. I'd keep both the toothbrushes to myself for that attitude, but really, that's just punishing me, isn't it?"

Both eyebrows were raised now. "Are we camping here for a while?"

Bear nodded. "I need time to make a plan and we're safe here for the time being."

She put the glass down on the counter. "What's your name?"

"It doesn't matter."

"I'm afraid it does. Or would you prefer me to keep calling you Pretty Boy?"

He ground his teeth. "Bear."

She slipped from her chair and walked around the corner. "Bear? Well, isn't that a fitting name. You are a big bear of a man, after all. Do you shift into one, too?"

He ignored the flash of pain her question inflicted. "My twin and I started using the literal translations of our actual names when we were teenagers."

"Why?"

He shrugged. "Uncontrolled angst? Hormone-induced protest? Teenaged rebellion? It was stupid, but it stuck, and now we're stuck with the names. Guess the joke was on us." Why in the Underworld did he share this story with her? She didn't need to know.

"And what's your twin's name? Flower?"

He clamped his lips together. Why'd she assume his twin was female? This was the second time she'd mentioned a sister when he hadn't said a thing. Had he? No. He was sure he hadn't. He might be drawn to this woman, but he'd never give up Raven. Twins before wins he always said, and he meant it.

"Ahh...you're protective. That's admirable." She smiled and kept walking closer, magic flowing out in delicious wave. "Protective and despite being a thief, you have a code of honour."

"Don't make me into a hero." He hated how her words hit him like slaps of cold water. He didn't deserve any praise. He'd broken into a secure compound and stolen a person for fuck's sake.

"I'm not." She smiled.

He wanted to go to her, gather her in his arms and lose himself in the sweet floral scent of her skin and chase away these feelings of failure. Instead, he stepped out of her path and placed the bags down on the coffee table.

Her lips quirked up as if she found his behaviour incredibly amusing or telling. "So, what shall we do with all this time?" Her dark gaze roamed his body.

"Not that."

"Why not? I've been cooped up in a magical box for fifty years."

"F...fifty years?"

"Some creative stretching would be good and having you with me will make it more fun." She winked.

"This is getting repetitive." He shut down the naughty images his brain tried to send him. "You need to stop trying to work your dark fae lust vibes on me."

She laughed, the trilling tinkle of bells. "Oh, that's so funny. You *still* think I'm doing this."

"Well, I know it's not my winning personality."

Chloe's expression grew serious. "You refused to hand me over to a dark fae lord even though this decision will result in a lost paycheque and quite possibly death."

"I didn't do this to get in your pants," Bear growled.

Chloe ignored him and continued. "You have turned down my repeated advances when most men would've leapt at the opportunity."

He didn't like the idea of other men and he definitely didn't like thinking about why he didn't like it.

"And then there's your magic."

Bear grunted.

"It woke me up like a warm ray of sunshine sneaking through the blinds after a night filled with thunderstorms. And I bet you're still denying the amount of power welling up within you, too."

"You're messing with me." She kept saying he had magic, but how would she sense it? His mind kept tripping over her claims from earlier. The charmed ring Marcus gave him obscured his magic and he hadn't taken it off. If magical wards couldn't sense his power, how could she?

The truth was she lied. Like all fae.

She shook her head and stepped closer, bringing her sweet scent with her. "I know you're part dark fae because of the magic behind that charm. Oh, don't give me that look. One of my special talents is seeing through such things. I told you, I bring light to where there's darkness. I see past all the camouflage. You have power and it's not just hiding behind that ring, is it? You've built a wall around it."

That stupid wall again, the one built from trauma. Bear clamped his mouth shut and refused to comment.

She shrugged. "You also have a twin, and you're protective of your sister. Oh hush, it has to be that way. One male, one female, two sides of the same coin. Powerful fae are always born as twins, as soulmates."

He balked. Gross. "She is *not* my soulmate."

"Soulmates for fae aren't the same as the soulmates you hear about in the movies or read in books. They're not what the werewolves pine after. When powerful dark fae are born, like you and your sister, the souls are formed to complement each other and balance the power. Your magic strengthens one another. Just as distance weakens you."

Guilt stabbed at his chest. Again. He really was an asshole. Raven was a shifter, but instead of shifting into one bird, she shifted into a whole bunch of them. She'd mentioned her conspiracy had grown smaller, but he'd never made the connection with him moving to the North Shore and withdrawing from family events, nor to his own power appearing to dwindle.

Chloe nodded, somehow reading him like a book. "I see that last one struck a nerve."

"Yeah, well, something or someone fucked up with the whole balancing thing, because my sister got almost all of it, while I got none."

Chloe cocked her head and reached out.

Bear flinched away, but she ignored him and slid her smooth hand along the side of his cheek and peered into his eyes. "You are so much more than what you see."

He grumbled.

"Let me show you."

"This seduction thing needs to stop."

She laughed again, and he wanted to keep saying things to make her laugh and it made no sense. He should be annoyed or angry. But he wasn't. At least not at Chloe.

"What do you suggest instead?" She dropped her hand and looked in the bag. "Cards?"

He shrugged. "Or we could watch some movies."

The overhead light caught the mischievous gleam in her eye. "Why don't we do it all? It will take a while for the fae to lose interest in finding the Claíomh Solais.

Plenty of time for me to seduce you with my *dark fae lust vibes*."

"You can try."

Her full mouth split into a wide grin. "Oh, I will."

Tasha took this opportunity to swoop into the apartment through an open window and land on the table near them.

Chloe stepped back, eyes wide. "Who's this?"

Bear reached forward and scratched the back of the bird's neck. "I call her Tasha."

"A pet?"

Tasha preened under the attention and stretched her neck.

"No, not a pet. A friend, maybe? She follows me whenever I'm outside."

"Like a shadow," Chloe whispered.

Something in her tone made Bear look up. Emotion flickered in her gaze, but Chloe hid it too quickly for Bear to decipher.

If he was being honest, he couldn't read women. He never doubted when he pissed off one of his sisters, but that skill probably developed from repeated exposure over his lifetime. Bear wasn't stupid, and his sisters were about as subtle as sledgehammers to the head.

The women he formed casual relationships with were different. Sure, he could read body language in the bedroom and decipher the physical stuff—when they liked or wanted something. He was attentive in bed and made sure they enjoyed their time with him. But the emotional, feely, frou-frou stuff? Not his strength. And it never bothered Bear that he lacked this skill.

Until now.

He wanted to rip apart the shield Chloe quickly constructed to hide her feelings. Tear it down, read her like a book, and make everything better. And not just with his dick, which was weird.

And new.

And uncomfortable.

Bear grunted and stepped away from Chloe. What in the Underworld was going on with him? He looked around for answers, but Chloe was too busy telling Tasha how pretty she was, and Tasha was too busy revelling in the attention.

Chloe reached out with her hand, pausing a few inches from Tasha. The bird stopped preening and cocked her head.

Bear held his breath. Tasha had never revealed herself to anyone outside his family before and she only let Bear or Raven touch her.

Instead of shying away, the bird hopped along the table and shoved her head into Chloe's hand.

Chloe obligingly scratched Tasha. She beamed at Bear over the bird, her smile dazzling.

Something weird happened in Bear's chest and he wasn't entirely sure he liked it.

Chapter Thirteen

"I have not failed. I've just found 10 000 ways that won't work."

~ *Thomas A. Edison*

A long strand of hair tickled Bear's face. He startled awake and jerked up. His forehead smacked against something solid. Ouch.

"Mmmph." Chloe reeled back and clutched her nose.

Bear threw off a blanket and sat up. Cool night air gently flowed through an open window, a nice refreshing change from the hot day spent cooped up inside. He winced and rubbed his forehead. The soft lamp light illuminated the couch and reflected off the blank television screen while casting Chloe in shadows. Her white hair cascaded down her body, clinging to her curves.

"You sure know how to thank a lady." Chloe straightened and dropped her hand from her nose. It wasn't bleeding and pain no longer crinkled her eyes. Instead, her gaze blazed from fire within, eyelids lowered, cheeks flushed, and mouth parted. He'd have to be a statue not to react to that look. Had she been anyone else, if this had been anywhere else, he would've reached out and pulled her to him. Every inch of his body wanted her right now, to sink into her heat and lose himself in the tangle of their bodies. Tension gripped him.

He shook his head. Not real. Stupid dark fae lust vibes.

"Sorry about the head butt. Reflexes. You okay?"

She grunted and sat down beside him. "I can see how you'd need to be vigilant with someone trying to cover you with a blanket."

Vigilant. He was a mockery of the word. It had been over a week of hiding and although the scratches on his face and his hand had healed, he was no closer to figuring out a solution to this mess. Instead, he'd grown closer to Chloe and complacent. Last night, he'd fallen asleep with her in his arms. He didn't pull away. He didn't extract himself. Oh, no. Not this idiot. He'd stayed and enjoyed the comforting sensation of her pressed against him and her hair in his face. Tonight, he'd fallen asleep on the couch again and this time hadn't stirred when Chloe got up, apparently. He was losing his touch.

"Oh, relax. It was just a blanket."

He glanced at the runes that kept her prisoner in the apartment. If the runes didn't prevent her from harming him, her own common sense would. Without him, she'd have no connection to the outside. Hmm. Was that the only reason he still drew breath?

"You mentioned the runes worked in a way I didn't understand," he said.

Her lips twitched.

"Why don't you explain them to me?"

Chloe leaned back on the couch. "I think not, Pretty Boy."

This wasn't the first time he'd asked, and like the other times, she refused to answer. "Why not?"

"I find watching this play out much more entertaining."

"Hmm."

She giggled and the tiny bells of her laughter spread warmth through his chest. What the in the Underworld was wrong with him?

"Bear?" She turned to him, her arm brushing his own.

"Yes, Chloe?"

She leaned toward him, her serious expression turning her face to stone.

The door burst open. Splinters flew through the air

and the door crashed into the wall. Dark fae soldiers poured into the room.

Bear sprang from the couch and lunged at the first soldier, blocking his strike and countering. His fist slammed into solid armour. Pain shot up his arm and he winced. He stepped out of the way, grabbing the man's arm and twisting it behind him. Before he could use it as leverage, a gauntlet covered fist smashed into his face.

Lights flashed.

Something cold pierced his side.

Bear staggered, crashing against a side table and knocking it over. He deflected more blows, barely reacting in time while he frantically searched the room. Chloe fought beside him, but there were too many of them.

"Run!" he yelled, ducking out of the way of another attack. He kicked the soldier out of the way. "Get out of here."

She shot him an annoyed glance and kept blocking her attacker's strikes. She was breathtaking. Spinning, dodging, ducking. She was a whirlwind of deflections and efficient counterstrikes. Heat poured off her.

Another fist broke through his guard and slammed into his side.

Oomph. The strike knocked the air from his lungs. He doubled over. A lamp crashed to the ground. Furniture flipped over. Too many.

He gushed blood. He'd been stabbed at least once. His vision wavered. They were going to die here—in his shitty safe house apartment with two glasses, two plates, a bowl and three spoons. And it was all his fault.

Bear continued to deflect blows as the soldiers continued to press forward. They hadn't drawn their swords—too cramped. He reached for his corvid energy and pulled. Desperate and grasping, he yanked at everything he had. Magic tore through him and he roared. The call of corvids filled the room, shattering glass and shaking the walls. Birds streamed into the apartment through the open windows, answering his call. They flew at the soldiers, pecking at faces, scraping and tearing skin with their talons.

The soldiers thrashed at the air, batting at the crows and ravens with their fists and knives. Birds croaked and cawed, squawking and crying out as they flailed to the ground.

No! Not that. Not them, too.

Where's Tasha?

His gut sunk as he frantically searched for his shadow among the fallen birds. He didn't see her, but he didn't feel her energy pinging against his, either.

Out of the chaos, a soldier stepped in front of Bear and unsheathed his sword. Cold settled over Bear. This was it. This warrior would gut him right here, right now.

"That's enough," a silky-smooth, melodious voice rang through the room, a woman's voice suggesting seduction and dark promises. Still enthralled by her voice, he wasn't prepared for corvid energy to crash against his. Intense, twisted and strangely alluring, the magic reached inside him, surrounded his power and squeezed. His energy suffocated.

The surviving crows and ravens called out in confusion, beady black eyes wild. They stopped attacking the fae while he struggled to breathe. Two soldiers stepped in behind Bear and gripped his arms. Two more soldiers did the same to Chloe. Now contained, the suffocating pressure on his corvid energy eased.

The soldiers at the door stepped aside to let a woman enter the room. Tall, lean, with black hair pulled back in intricate knots, her pale face emitted a light all on its own. She wore a dress made of black feathers that hugged the top of her body and flared out into a skirt at her hips. It didn't fit with the large metal scythe with a skull etched into the blade that she clutched in one hand.

"Poor choice of accessories," his youngest sister, Juni, would have said. Fuck, he was glad she was nowhere near here.

Bear panted, sweat running down his face and blood running down his body. He likely faced death in the next few minutes and all he could think about was his siblings and their snark.

He focused on the woman with the commanding presence. Her black eyes and suffocating power marked her as dark fae, but she also wore a subtle black crown barely noticeable in her mass of black braids.

"Who are you?" he asked.

A cruel smile spread across her face. "I'm Lloth,

Queen of Corvids, and you are...?"

Screwed. He was absolutely, one hundred percent screwed. His face must've said it all because the woman laughed. Unlike Chloe's tinkling laughter, he had no wish to hear any more of this woman's cackling.

"I know your name, Bjorn Crawford. I've been looking for you. I've even met your sister."

Though he had two sisters, he knew automatically which one she referred to. "Stay away from Raven."

She leaned forward. "No."

Bear lunged at her, but the firm grips on his arms kept him in place. He looked around the room, desperately, frantically, searching for escape. If he could shift like Raven, he'd already be out of the room and Chloe wouldn't have stayed. His abdomen ached with a painful throb.

"You should've run," he told Chloe.

She shook her head, white hair clumped together with sweat and blood.

Lloth snorted. She pointed at the runes drawn on the wall. "She couldn't leave when she's bound to you."

Bear groaned. He was an idiot. In the middle of fighting for his life, he'd forgotten about the runes locking Chloe in the apartment.

"She could've broken the spell quite easily, of course," Lloth continued. "I find it interesting that she didn't."

Bear's heart sank. He didn't need help filling in the blanks. He knew he couldn't trust the fae, even if he was half fae himself. He scowled and turned to Chloe. "So, that's why you were so drawn to me, huh?"

Anger flashed across Chloe's face. Not quite the emotion he'd expected.

Lloth laughed and stepped forward. He struggled against the other men's holds, but they forced him onto his knees as the queen approached.

"You are pretty." She reached out, cupped his chin and forced his face up. "Pretty stupid."

Huh?

"She didn't need to seduce her way out of the spell created by the runes. She couldn't. To release herself, all she had to do was kill you."

Shock spread through his body so fast he froze. What?

"And despite your impressive combat skills, mortal, the Claíomh Solais, the White Glaive of Light, the bastard daughter of Erebus, God of Darkness, has a few generations of practice on you."

He gaped at Chloe. She could've killed him at any time. Unease clamped his spine. Chloe could've killed him twenty minutes ago when he fell asleep on the couch.

Lloth's smile was wicked and cruel. "She could've escaped at any time."

Chloe's angry gaze burned the side of his face. She'd spared him instead of escaping. Maybe her attraction to him wasn't a lie after all. But that meant...

He shook his head. No. He wasn't the kind of person to swoon over a beautiful woman. There had to be more going on here.

"She found you special." Lloth leaned down and stroked his face with her free hand. "And I think I know why."

Bear used to want to be special. He wanted to stand out. Impress. Be that guy other men wanted to be and the women wanted to fuck.

Not anymore.

Any remaining ambition to be stand out from the crowd fled from the gleam in Lloth's gaze.

And his change of heart wouldn't matter. He could protest and deny and nothing would spare him from this moment. This fate.

She'd take him anyway.

Chapter Fourteen

"The way I see it, if you want the rainbow, you gotta put up with the rain."

~ *Dolly Parton*

The large warriors threw Bear into a prison cell. With a black bag over his head, he couldn't see anything to confirm his suspicions, but the air smelled stale, the ground was hard and there was a lot of metal clanking before he flew through the air. His body smacked the floor, then his head, with a loud crack. Pain flared behind his eyes and a sharp ache throbbed along the side of his body.

The impact with the hard concrete floor knocked the wind out of him. With his hands bound, he couldn't break his fall. One moment he was jostled down some steps, then with the creak of metal hinges as his only warning, Bear became weightless, to flop in the air like a fish hauled out of water.

Now firmly pressed against cold concrete or tile, Bear lay motionless, sucking in air and trying to get his breath back.

Someone roughly rolled him over and fiddled with his shackles. Bound, gagged and sort-of blindfolded, things weren't looking good for Bear.

The memory of the psychotic sparkle in Lloth's gaze did nothing to reassure him of his future prospects.

Something landed beside him with a loud thump. Chloe groaned.

Assholes.

They didn't need to handle her so roughly.

Anger rose inside him, his power welled.

Metal clanked as they likely shackled Chloe to the floor as they had with him.

One of the warriors ripped the black hood from Bear's head. He blinked repeatedly until his vision adjusted to the change in lighting. Low burning lanterns, flickering firelight in a dark room confirmed his thoughts. Yup. A jail cell. But not a dingy one, at least.

As far as dungeons went, Bear had little experience to draw on, but this barren dry space didn't fit the picture he had in his mind. The dusty floors and windowless rooms didn't make for a comfortable stay, sure, but there weren't skeletal husks of former prisoners, rats, or random dripping sounds either.

The warrior who'd almost gutted him earlier leaned down with a cruel smile. "Don't worry," he said. "You won't be here long."

Bear swallowed. Things were definitely not looking good for him. He should've told that dark fae client to fuck off right from the start. He would still be completing more jobs for the guild, blissfully unaware of the details of Lloth's dungeon.

He hesitated and looked over at Chloe. She'd straightened to a sitting position and glared at the warrior.

Unease gnawed at his gut.

If he hadn't taken this job, he wouldn't have met Chloe. Someone else would've stolen the Claíomh Solais. They probably would've listened to the orders, too, and not opened the box. They would've handed it over without realizing what it contained. There was the rub.

His gut twisted more. Stomach acid bubbled up his throat. This wasn't the first time he'd had this thought. He wouldn't wish that fate for Chloe, even if it meant this fate for him.

He glanced over at her again and the weird collar they'd clamped around her neck leaked with dark magic.

The warrior backed away and the other guards parted to let Lloth enter the jail cell. The long skirt of her dress whispered against the stones. The crazy gleam in her gaze was still there.

"What my caomhnóir means to say is that you won't be here long because you'll soon be mine."

Well, that wasn't happening.

Lloth stepped closer and laughed. "Oh, you might feel defiant now, but I can be very convincing."

Chloe sucked in a breath. "Lloth, no. I'll do what you want. Take me but leave him out of this."

Warmth spread through his chest and then panic stabbed him. Lloth couldn't have Chloe. No one could. She was...his?

He shook his head. No. That wasn't right.

Chloe belonged to herself. But he wanted her to be his.

The realization hit him harder than any of Lloth's soldiers and air rushed from his lungs all over again.

The Corvid Queen turned her attention to Chloe. "And why would I do that, when I can have you both?"

"He's just a thief," Chloe said.

Ouch. That hurt. She wasn't wrong, but Bear thought...Bear hoped... Argh. Bear was a dumbass. And it didn't matter what he thought.

Lloth chuckled and her lips curled into another smile. "Oh, I think we both know he's so much more than that."

Chloe's head snapped back as if Lloth's words physically slapped her.

"I've changed my mind." Lloth straightened and jerked her chin in Bear's direction. "I'm not waiting for tomorrow. Bring him now."

Chapter Fifteen

"To the person who has my voodoo doll: please give it a rest."

~ *Bear Crawford*

Bear's back slammed onto a cold metal table. Lanterns flickered their golden light against the stone walls but offered little in the way of warmth.

The warrior, the one she called her keev-noy-er or whatever, leaned over the table, gripped Bear's shirt and tore it free from his body. The material cut into his skin as the man yanked it away.

"You're not my type," Bear said.

The warrior dropped the remains of Bear's shirt on the floor and punched him in the face.

Bear's head snapped back and slammed into the table. His ears rung. The keev-noy-er hadn't hit him full force—he'd be knocked out cold if he had—but it still hurt.

Bear shut his mouth, probably what the keev-noy-er wanted.

Lloth flowed into the small room like smoke on a dance floor, and probably just as toxic. She stepped up to Bear's other side, across from the warrior. "We need him healthy."

"You need him alive," the warrior grumbled.

Lloth chuckled, but her expression turned serious the moment her attention refocused on Bear. "Take them out."

"What?"

"You have some awful contraption covering your eyes. Take them out."

His brain scrambled to make sense of her demand. "My...contacts?"

She waved her hand in the air as if terminology was of no importance. "Yes, those. Why do you wear them? Fae don't suffer vision impairment."

"I'm only half fae."

She snorted as if that didn't make a difference and he had the sudden urge to yell at her. He didn't wear the contacts to correct his vision. He wore them to hide. Lloth had no idea what it was like to lie about who she was. Her dismissiveness grated his nerves.

Bear nearly choked on his conflicting feelings when he was younger—confused whether to feel shame for being something others considered disgusting, weak for feeling the all-to-real fear of what regs would do if they discovered what he was, or guilt for hiding instead of proudly announcing his ancestry. Sometimes, like right now, he felt like a fraud—claiming a heritage he didn't fully understand and certainly didn't have the power to back it up.

"Why?" Lloth pushed.

"To hide my eyes from regs," he said. Black eyes easily identified him as dark fae.

Lloth frowned at him. "Why would you hide what you are from those pathetic fools? You are more than what any of them could ever be."

"Well, there's more of them than me and they don't exact harbour any warm fuzzy feelings for half-fae." And a lack-lustre power-poor one at that. He would be vulnerable to any attack. Man, did she have the wrong guy.

Lloth narrowed her eyes and leaned closer. "Either you take them out, or I will." She waggled her fingers in the air, her long dark pointed nails glistening under the lantern light.

Yeah, fuck that. He raised his shackled hands and shook them to rattle the chains. When they'd hauled him from the cell, they'd rebound his hands in front of his body instead of behind. While his shoulders enjoyed the relief, the whole being shackled thing was becoming old fast.

Lloth jerked her chin at the keev-noy-er.

"And something to wash my hands?" he asked.

Lloth scowled at him. "Did my caomhnóir hit your head too hard? Did you wake up and suddenly think you were in a spa? We're not here to serve you."

"My hands are dirty. I've listened to the women in my family nag me my whole life about eyes being the primary site of infections. I need to wash my hands before I touch my face." He paused and shrugged. "Unless you want me to get sick?"

Lloth's gaze flashed. "Oh, yes. The Crawford women. We'll talk about them soon enough. One in particular."

Bear snapped his mouth shut. Fuck.

Lloth sighed and waved her hand in the air. The keev-noy-er grunted and stalked off, presumably to get Bear something to wash his hands with.

"You won't be smiling for long, Bjorn Crawford."

"What's a keev-noy-er?" he asked, wanting to change the topic away from his impending torture.

"A keev-noy-er?" Lloth's mouth turned down.

Bear nodded toward the door the warrior had left through.

Lloth followed his gaze and her face relaxed. "A caomhnóir involves a sacred bond. One I will not discuss with you."

The caomhnóir stomped back into the room with a bowl full of water and a face cloth. When he reached Bear, he shoved them in his direction.

Bear sat up and washed his hands. He took his time, spreading the pathetic lather of the dense soap over his forearms like he was preparing for surgery, until his fingertips grew numb.

"That's enough," Lloth hissed.

Bear shook his hands out over the bowl and looked at the caomhnóir expectantly. "Towel?"

"Fuck off."

Bear sighed and pulled the contacts from his dry eyes. The soap still lingering on his fingertips stung. He squeezed his eyes shut while they continued to sting and water.

"Aww look, he's choking up." The caomhnóir's snide remark with fake concern made Bear want to punch him in the face.

The caomhnóir stepped back, out of reach, as if reading Bear's intent. Getting one more shot in before the torture started would've been nice. Bear let the contacts fall to the ground. No point hanging onto them.

The man scanned Bear's body. "We need to tend those wounds first if we're going to do this now. He might bleed out on us."

Lloth sighed and spoke over her shoulder to one of the other guards. "Bring the healer."

"You're going to heal me so you can break me?" Bear asked. That made no sense.

"Precisely." Lloth's full lips quirked. She'd be a beautiful woman if she weren't intent on hurting him.

The guard returned with a gnarled old woman. She

shuffled into the room and scowled at everyone, including the queen. No one corrected her insolence.

The healer stepped up to the table. Her scowl softened briefly when she looked over the mess of his torso. She jabbed the angry skin near one of the stab wounds. The sympathetic expression quickly disappeared, replaced with a determined frown. "He'll live."

"I know that, you foolish woman. Stop the bleeding so he survives what I have planned."

"Who pissed in your cornflakes?" Bear asked. What possible reason did Lloth have to speak to the old woman that way? Mom would tear a strip off his hide if she ever caught him disrespecting an elderly person this way.

Unless it was their crazy neighbour, but Mrs. Humphreys was an exception.

Lloth turned her unsettling black gaze on him.

He instantly regretted saying anything.

"When you have your heart ripped out and shredded apart for everyone to see and laugh at, then you'll have an infinitesimal speck of understanding for the pain I harbour inside."

Okay, then...

Mental note. If he survived this, he needed to make sure none of his exes visited Lloth in the Underworld. They didn't need any ideas.

The old woman patted his stomach as if to say, "there, there."

"Just get on with it," Lloth hissed.

The woman nodded, placed both her gnarled hands on Bear's torso and hummed. Heat spread through his chest. His skin prickled and the stab wounds stung. The urge to leap up and run away tugged at his muscles. Blood rushed through his body to pool near the injuries. Flesh knitted together. The odd sensation wasn't exactly painful, but it wasn't pleasant either.

The woman wavered on her feet and withdrew her hands to grip the table. When she stopped swaying, she opened her eyes. "It's done."

"Now we can begin," Lloth said.

The old woman hobbled away, slipping from the room and into the darkness without another word while the guards closed in around the table. Not even a thank you.

Jerks.

Rough hands pushed Bear back. He swung at the warrior but missed. And just like that, he was flat on his back looking up at Lloth and her caomhnóir as they leaned over him.

Lloth began to mumble some dark fae words. It was all gibberish to Bear. The caomhnóir held out another bowl. He must've prepared it while Bear had his healing session. The slop smelled like mud.

Lloth grabbed a black-handled brush resting in it. Dark paint coated the coarse wide-angled bristles, too black to be mud. The smell intensified, bringing hints of iron with it.

Lloth continued her mumbling chant as she drew runes on Bear's chest. The cold paint sent chills along his skin.

The other guards moved into place and shackled his legs and arms to the table.

Bear didn't struggle. What was the point? He wouldn't escape this room alive. Not right now. He had no delusions regarding his fighting prowess. Bear needed to conserve his energy to survive whatever Lloth had planned and then escape when the opportunity presented itself.

Lloth's chanting grew louder and the cold paint grew colder and colder until it burned. As if she took a poker to his skin and branded him like cattle, the runes dug into his flesh. The smell of burnt meat filled the room.

Bear had planned to stay silent. He'd planned to be strong, be brave. Those plans quickly changed. Sweat coated his body, along with paint and blood. Bear screamed. His shouts echoed in the room with Lloth's constant chanting acting like some sort of backbeat. If his body couldn't flee, maybe his mind could. His thoughts frantically searched for somewhere else to go.

Lloth slapped his face. His cheeks stung and his vision refocused on her cruel smile. Her dark magic coated him, saturating his skin and soaking in like some sort of evil body mask.

"Let me in," she said.

Hard pass. His magic recoiled from her touch, drawing in farther and farther into himself, behind the crumbled walls he'd spent a lifetime making.

The pain intensified. His heart thumped fast and

irregular. His mind spiralled into childhood memories. Teasing his twin, Mom kissing his booboos, visiting the hospital to meet his baby brother for the first time, holding Juni in his arms. Giggles and laughter. Tears and crying. Family. Terry holding him and telling him everything was going to be okay after Raven shifted and he didn't. Bear had broken down sobbing, the disappointment overwhelming.

Then another memory. A recent one. Mischievous black eyes. Skin as soft as silk and dark as night. White hair cascading around the most beautiful face he'd ever seen, like moonlight spilling over a lake at midnight. Open eyes that pierced through him and saw him for who he truly was.

"Stop fighting me." Lloth pushed her magic deeper.

Bear retreated again, scrambling back, building his barriers as he had before.

Lloth screamed, her frustration palpable. The magic broke across the room. Deadly silence fell over them, only Bear's panting echoed in the room now.

"My queen?" her caomhnóir spoke after a few minutes.

Lloth growled and clutched the table. Her nails filed into claws grated against the metal. "Take him back to the cell. I'll try again tomorrow."

The promise in her voice did little to settle the chill running along his spine.

Chapter Sixteen

"To get the full value of joy you must have someone to divide it with."

~ *Mark Twain*

Lloth retrieved Bear from the cell again and again and again. Each time, Lloth drew her runes on him with black paint, chanted in dark fae and made his body contort with pain. Each time, his mind drifted to memories of his family or Chloe. Each time, Lloth finished the session by growling in frustration and cursing his name. Each time, the caomhnóir threw Bear into the cell unceremoniously and shackled him to the cold floor like a misbehaving dog. And each time, after the guards left, Chloe would use what power she could still access with the magical collar on to warm him.

Bear was losing his grip on reality. He slipped in and out of consciousness. How many days and nights had they spent as Lloth's prisoners? Had it been two days? Or two hundred? He didn't know.

"Try to use your power," Chloe whispered.

He flinched away from the sound of her voice. Was she even real? Or had Lloth created an illusion to trick him? To get him to open up, to become unguarded.

"Can't," he said. "Must keep it hidden."

The heat radiating off Chloe intensified. "They won't be back for a while. You need to embrace your power."

He shook his head and instantly regretted it. Pain throbbed behind his eyes and his stomach rolled. He swallowed repeatedly, forcing the stomach acid back down his throat, and waited until his vision stopped swimming.

"You've drawn too much into yourself. It's part of what's making you sick."

He clenched his hands into fists. The shackles bit into raw skin. He'd thrown out his original plans to conserve energy. He'd tried to fight back. He'd struggled against the guards. He tried to get away. He even tried to get them to kill him—anything to avoid the pain *she* planned.

"Trust me," Chloe whispered.

"Are you real?"

The heat of her magic intensified in answer. Of course, she was real. Lloth couldn't imitate sincere warmth like this.

He shut his eyes and opened the gates his power hid behind. Lloth had taken his ring, but he didn't need it to protect his magic. Every time Lloth had made a grab for his power, he'd retreated farther into himself— farther than he'd ever pulled his magic back before.

He let his essence trickle out, like a new stream running through drought-ridden soil, the magic soaked into each crack and crevice. The energy vibrating in his cells soothed the chafed feeling from his sessions with Lloth and acted like a balm to the throbbing pain. He let out more and more, until his body became flooded with power, every cell soaked, his skin and soul drenched.

"Beautiful," Chloe said.

Bear let the magic well inside and tilted his head back. In a sudden burst, he made a call—the call of corvids. He knew no one would answer him. Not here. Not locked in the dungeons and sequestered away within an intricate fortress.

Energy pinged against his.

Bear straightened.

What in the Underworld?

More energy pinged.

Ravens, crows, magpies. So many corvids.

Warmth spread across his chest. The birds couldn't come to him, but they answered his call with their own magic to comfort him.

My pretties, he told them. *Thank you.*

Something clicked at the end of the hall.

Bear clammed up and snuffed out his power. His muscles ached and his heart whined at the sudden loss, but he couldn't risk the guards witnessing his magic or Lloth detecting it.

The clicking drew closer. The dungeon was too dark for him to see well past the bars of the cell, but the clicking was too quiet to come from one of Lloth's heavy-footed guards.

He straightened into a sitting position and leaned forward.

Tasha hopped into view. An ordinary raven, sleek and black and perfect in every way. Such a silly thing to want to cry over, yet, emotion welled behind his eyes.

"Hey, girl."

The bird held a piece of bread in its beak.

"Persistent little thing," Chloe said. "She must've snuck past the guard."

"Hey, Tasha." Bear smiled at the bird. His voice was scratchy and raw from all the screaming. "You found me. Again. How'd you get in here?"

The bird cocked her head at him, poked her beak through the bars and dropped the bread into the cell. She sent images of him eating.

"Thank you," Bear said. "You're such a sweet thing. But you shouldn't be here."

She sent him a feeling of warmth. He didn't

understand at first, she usually communicated with images. It took him a moment to realize she was sending him her love. His eyes stung.

"Oh, you charmer." He sent her back the warm feeling he always got in his chest when he thought about her.

Tasha clicked happily and hopped up and down.

"I think I might be jealous," Chloe said.

Tasha clicked at her.

"You naughty thing." His words made her click even more, a black ball of excitement.

The door slammed open at the end of the hall. Heavy footsteps pounded against the stone floor. Joy quickly curdled into dread. Bear's stomach churned. This couldn't be happening.

"Get out of here," Bear hissed and waved his hands frantically at Tasha. She couldn't be caught, too. "Go!"

The raven croaked and launched into the air—right into the gauntlet covered hand of Lloth's caomhnóir. The warrior closed his hand around the struggling Tasha while carrying a plate of food in his other hand.

Bear stopped breathing.

He'd beg if he thought it would help. But he couldn't let the guard know Tasha meant anything to him. She might have a chance if the asshole believed she was just another bird.

His stomach twisted tighter.

Lloth's caomhnóir studied the raven in his grip. He tossed the food onto the floor and kicked it into Bear's cell without looking. The metal plate clattered along the concrete, spilling the meager portion of rice all over.

Tasha continued to struggle, flapping her wings and scratching at the warrior's armour with her talons. Beady eyes flicked to Bear, begging for help.

"Ah." The caomhnóir leaned toward the bird.

The raven tried to peck at his face.

He responded with a cruel smile, holding the bird far enough away to avoid contact. "A traitor."

He finally turned to Bear, his smile spreading. "This is what we do to traitors."

"No!" Bear lurched forward. The shackles clanked and held him in place. "Please, no." He strained toward Tasha. He thrashed against the restraints. His girl. His shadow. "I'll do anything. Please. Don't do this. I'll do what you want."

"You'll do what we want anyway." The caomhnóir clenched his fist and used his thumb to break Tasha's neck. Bones snapped, her head bent at an awkward angle.

"Nooooooo!" The tension knotted in his gut released into a wave of nausea. Bear slumped where he sat. He watched helplessly as the guard tossed the lifeless body into the cell. Tasha flopped against the cold stone floor, falling in a pile of scattered rice.

"Tasha," Bear whispered. Something inside him broke.

The caomhnóir chuckled and walked away, his footsteps growing lighter and more distant with each step.

Bear crumpled forward, his face a few feet away from the Tasha. Her last moments were filled with fear and confusion, wondering why he didn't help.

He couldn't save her.

He couldn't even hold her.

"I'm so sorry," Chloe whispered, voice cracking.

He heard her words and felt the heat of her magic against his skin, her way of trying to comfort him. But inside, he felt nothing.

Chapter Seventeen

"The loss is immeasurable, but so is the love left behind."

~ Unknown

Bear woke up with his bruised face smushed against cold concrete. How long had he been like this? How long had Lloth held him in the dungeons? Beating him? Drawing on him like some psychotic street performer? Whispering words of magic and getting angry when he didn't respond the way she wanted. She seemed to gain new motivation since Tasha...Since Tasha.

Each night, or day, or hour, Lloth had her guards throw him back in this prison cell, disgusted and angry.

Bear may have lost track of time and space, but he'd never forget the soothing words from Chloe. Too incoherent to reply, he relished the words of encouragement. He clung to words speaking of respect, pride and love, though the last emotion didn't quite make sense. How could she love him? A thief. A coward. A talentless hack. And now, a prisoner. A man so weak, he lost all sense of himself when the big bad guard killed a bird.

His stomach sunk. Tasha wasn't just a bird. She was his friend and constant companion, and had been for years. Even when everything else around him turned to shit, she was always there.

The energy of the Underworld rolled over him and strummed the runes covering his skin. Lloth had drawn different runes on him this time and though he felt nothing change during her babbling—pain was pain— she'd cackled with glee when the torture session ended. Frankly, he was beginning to think this Corvid Queen wasn't mentally stable.

Chloe moaned beside him and rolled over. She hadn't been beaten like him but sleeping on the cold stone floor with minimal food, listening to him suffer and being given no guarantee of a future took its own toll on her as well. They must've dragged her out at some point as well because she now had runes drawn on her, too. They looked different than his, but Bear wasn't an expert on runes.

He turned toward her. They'd allowed them to stay in the same cell the entire time despite the neighbouring ones appearing empty, but they'd chained them so they couldn't touch. Why had they done that? Some sick form of torture?

Bear's shackles clinked against the stone floor and prevented him from reaching out. Bear wasn't a wordsmith. He didn't spout pretty poetry and express his feelings well. Or at all. But he wanted to hold her, to soothe away the pain etched on her face like her words had comforted him. For the first time since Lloth's caomhnóir killed Tasha, he could think, and hopefully speak, clearly.

He looked around and discovered someone had removed Tasha's body—probably chucking her out like unwanted waste. He swallowed the lump in his throat. He needed to keep a clear head.

Chloe struggled to sit up. She shuffled around on her butt to face him. "I'm glad to see you're doing better. This is the first time you've sat up in a while."

"You must think I'm weak."

"Why would you say that?"

"Tasha." His mouth stumbled over the name.

She narrowed her eyes and balled her hands into fists. "That man is vile and cruel. He lacks any empathy or compassion. I don't think you're weak for having a heart. I cried for that sweet thing, too."

Bear bowed his head. He had been so lost in his own pain and grief he hadn't noticed hers. He really was a selfish jerk. He kept finding reasons for pushing Chloe away and she'd done nothing to deserve it. If she'd killed him in his apartment and ran, she wouldn't even be here.

"Why?" Bear croaked, his voice raw from screaming. "Why didn't you escape?"

Silence answered him. Bound by thick metal and imprisoned somewhere in the Underworld in Lloth's dungeon, he had nowhere to go. He waited.

"I was drawn to you," she muttered after a long uncomfortable silence.

"I could have sold you out. I could've finished the job and handed you over. You had no way of knowing what I'd do or what I was capable of. You didn't know me. Why risk it?"

She shrugged and looked away. "It's been a long time, Pretty Boy, since I've been drawn to anything. The risk was worth the prize."

He swallowed a lump in his throat. "So, it was real?"

She smiled, sadness and pain still pulling at her features. "It *is* real, yes. And mutual as I've tried to tell you often enough."

He sighed, some tension releasing from his body despite their circumstances. At least he made the right decision to open the box and not to hand Chloe over to the dark fae lord. If he'd refused to meet with the client...If the job had gone to someone else...

Ice flowed through his veins. He didn't like those thoughts or the feelings, they invoked. It hadn't happened that way so no point in dwelling on the possible past.

"What does she want with you?" he asked. "What do those runes do?"

"She wants what all fae want. More power." Chloe glanced down at the runes on her arms. "And I suspect revenge."

"Did you steal her man?"

She shook her head. "Her black shriveled heart got hurt and she believes I can give her the power to get back at the person she feels wronged her."

Bear grunted. Not all fae wanted power. At least he didn't. Not anymore. Since taking this job, he'd realized power wouldn't fill the hole he'd dug in his own soul from insecurities. When he looked at his own death in the cold, emotionless eyes of the dark fae queen and her sidekick, all he thought about was his family. And Chloe.

"I'm more worried about why she wants you," Chloe said, nodding at his chest.

"Do you know what they are?" The runes itched his skin and if his hands hadn't been bound, he would've rubbed his skin raw trying to get them off the second the guards left him.

"Yes."

He waited.

She glanced away and bit her lip.

"I'd rather know, Chloe."

She nodded and turned back to him. "They link your magic with hers. It's like an anam cara, but a forced defiled version of the bond."

"What the fuck is an anam cara?"

She shook her head. "It doesn't matter. Not right now. We don't have time to get into that. What you need to know is she's forged a connection with you, so she can force you to access your power."

That didn't sound good. "She's going to make me do bad things?"

"Yes, but...she couldn't make a true bond. You had to be willing for that, or at least compliant, and you fought her off." Something close to pride flashed across her expression. "That's why she went with this spell. It's not as good though. She can push you to use your powers and try to direct you." Chloe swallowed. "But she can't—"

The metal door to the dungeon wrenched open and guards walked down the hall toward them, their heavy armoured boots hitting the cold stones. The guards stopped in front of Bear. Cold dark eyes of the Underworld appraised him.

Lloth's caomhnóir stepped forward. "It's time."

Chapter Eighteen

"Light travels faster than sound. That's why some folks appear bright until they speak."

~ *Gary Apple*

Bear stumbled forward, unable to see a thing with the stupid black cloth bag over his head. The energy inside him pulsed stronger and stronger with each step, confirming he headed toward something, but he wasn't sure what. Another one of Lloth's torture sessions? Her big reveal of her master plan? The possibility of escape? This time was different than the other times they'd hauled him from the cell. This time he had the hood on, and they'd brought Chloe along. Dread twisted his gut at the possibilities.

He didn't want to become separated from Chloe. Whatever they faced, he wanted to face it together.

Hinges creaked ahead and fresh ocean air washed over him. The guards ushered him forward, their feet shuffling against the stone flooring. Red moonlight brightened the inside of the black hood. Ocean waves crashed nearby, and an overwhelming sensation of corvid energy hit him like a body shot. Lloth's now familiar power wound around him like a nauseating illness, but more corvid magic danced in the air. There must be hundreds of birds nearby, he sensed them with his inner eye and itched to call to them. But the most potent source of magic he felt in the room, the one he was most drawn to, was Raven's.

His twin sister was here.

He'd know the signature of her dark energy anywhere. It brushed against his own, strengthening his power as he drew closer. They stopped him beside Chloe, her floral scent comforting, though the distance between them was still too far.

What the fuck was his sister doing here? The only crime she'd ever committed in life was dating an epic douchebag years ago.

"Chloe." A man swore in a deep rumbling voice.

Bear stiffened. Who was that?

"You would use absolute light to control him?" his sister said. What was she talking about? Light couldn't control him.

"The brightest light casts the darkest shadow." Lloth's voice echoed in the room.

They sounded as if they spoke in riddles. Was any of this supposed to make sense?

Bear focused less on their words and tried to gather information on their surroundings. They must be in a large space and they weren't alone. Murmurings and mutterings of other people filled in the background sound.

"She cannot control Cole, she empowers him," Lloth continued. "The only reason Camhanaich doesn't rule this realm is because he chose not to, and it was my price for helping him. Now, I will harness his power and bolster my own claim."

Well, fuck. This wasn't about him at all. Who in the Underworld was Cole? Why had Lloth brought them to this show? What did she plan? More psychological torture? His mind reeled and he missed some of what was said.

Someone growled and boots slapped the stone flooring toward them. Who? What did they plan to do?

"Uh, uh, uh." Lloth scolded.

Chloe sucked in a breath, and without seeing, he knew Lloth had done something to her using magic. The power buzzed in the air. Those runes. They must allow Lloth to hurt her in some way.

That burning anger rose inside him again. If he got free, he'd make sure Lloth paid for every ounce of pain she inflicted on Chloe. He didn't believe in harming women, but he'd make an exception for this crazy bitch.

When had he grown so protective of Chloe? Right from the start? When he learned someone stuffed her into a magical box? He shuffled a half step closer to Chloe, so his arm pressed into hers. He might not be able to hold her, but he could let her know he was still here.

Chloe leaned into his arm, sending warmth through his body. Somehow, their situation didn't feel as dire as before.

"I'm so glad you understand the importance of twins," Lloth continued. "Imagine my delight when I arrived to retrieve Chloe and found a gem all of his own."

Wait. That was him.

"So ignorant to his own power, he hasn't learned how to wield it," Lloth said. "I could sense his twin nature immediately and Cole's reasons for hiding you became crystal clear. Your power is so unique I changed my plans."

Bear froze, now understanding why he'd been spared in the apartment and why they'd healed his stab wounds only to beat him again and draw runes all over his body. They didn't want him. They wanted to control Raven.

"You plan to threaten my brother to control me, too?" Raven's voice cracked.

Bear stiffened. He wanted to wrench himself from the bindings, tear off the hood and get her out of here.

Why was she here? How had she become involved? Had she tried to find him? He pushed forward and struggled against his bonds, but the guard behind him held him in place.

"Silly child." Lloth giggled. "I plan to destroy you and control him with your power."

No! The power within Bear surged, calling the corvids to him. He didn't sing or serenade them out loud this time. The call came from within. He swayed under the force of power flowing through him.

The guard tugged on his bound arms and he staggered away from Chloe. His arm grew cold from where he'd pressed against her. Bear ground his teeth, ignored the guard and pulled on his power more. The birds would do his bidding He'd force them to comply. It went against his nature to demand instead of ask, but he couldn't let Lloth harm Raven. He couldn't stand by while the Corvid Queen took out his twin.

So focused on drawing his power for Raven, he missed some of the conversation again. Lloth being crazy, no doubt.

"I will rip the corvid energy from her inferior body and leave your latest infatuation a dry husk." Lloth must be talking to someone else in the room. "You will serve me again. You will bow to my commands."

Bear growled. One of the guards punched him in the back. Bear lurched, but the guard's grip on his shackles prevented him from falling over. The guard ripped off his hood. Sudden light momentarily blinded him, and he blinked until his eyes adjusted. They stood in a grand hall, the walls opened up to the night sky instead of a ceiling. Pillars, walls and floor tiles made from some sort of black shiny stone shone under the red moonlight. Hundreds of birds perched on the ramparts and watched with their beady black eyes. Lloth stood at the head of the room, wielding the scary looking scythe and wearing another dress made of feathers. If pressed, Bear couldn't say exactly what made this outfit different from the last. It just was.

Fae lined the runway that led down to where his sister stood. If they didn't whisper in each other's ears or move their heads back and forth to study the queen and his sister, he would've mistaken them for statues. Fancy dressed statues.

At the other end of a long black runner, Raven defiantly faced Lloth. With messy black hair, some god-awful unflattering shorts and a shirt soaked with what appeared to be dried sweat and blood, Raven didn't look her best. Yet, she stood straight with her shoulders back, chin up and determination flashing in her gaze. Grandma Lu would've been proud to see her granddaughter offer defiance in the face of danger. If anyone could get them out of this, his twin could. She was the resourceful one of the bunch.

After scanning his face and body and evidently noting the injuries, Raven looked as though she wanted to murder someone. Her hands clenched into fists and her lips flattened. The power inside her built like a stoking fire. He pulled more of his own magic and fed her. He had no idea if it would work, but after Chloe talking about soulmates and Lloth being psychotic and planning to use him as a personal battery pack, he had to try something.

"Cole." Chloe's delicate voice drew Bear's attention away from his sister. He followed Chloe's gaze and choked. Shadow Man. The scary fae from the vault stood near his sister. Light where Chloe was dark, and dark where she was light, Shadow Man, or Cole, appeared the polar opposite of the woman standing beside him. Only his dark Other gaze resembled Chloe's—deep and powerful. Who was he to Chloe? Her captor? Her...lover?

While he had no answers to those questions, he knew who Cole was to Lloth—the one who broke her heart. He was the reason they were all in this mess. Bear's sister was in danger because of Cole, and so was Chloe.

Bear cringed.

No. That didn't sound quite right. Raven was here because of him. His twin got caught up in this clusterfuck because of his involvement.

"If only you stayed with me," Lloth said to Cole. Her lean figure swayed on the dais at the top of the stairs, as if she fed off the conflicting emotions in the room and found them overwhelming.

"Now you shall be mine for good." She flicked her finger at Chloe, and the runes flickered again. Chloe cried out.

Bear lunged to reach her, but the guards held him in place. He had little knowledge of runes, but Lloth's actions needed no explanation. She'd threatened Chloe's life. Shadow Man couldn't interfere with whatever she had planned.

Lloth held her hand out toward Bear. The runes on his skin glowed. Lloth's power twisted inside him, grasped his power and pushed.

Bear grunted.

Lloth swayed. The more Bear's runes glowed, the more he burned and the more she rocked. She pushed magic from his body, forcing him to use it, to silently call the corvids. The scythe in Lloth's hand shone. The energy inside him pulsed, calling more and more birds and corvid energy.

Ravens croaked as more corvids swooped into the room from the dark summer night above. More and more, they came in waves. Lloth pushed him harder, his hands shook, his body vibrated, but he kept calling the birds. Too transfixed with her spells and manipulation, she hadn't caught on to his intent, yet.

Connected to Lloth with these scribblings on his body, he sensed what she wanted. She planned to draw upon the power of the corvids he called, magically feeding off them. But she couldn't force the direction of his magic. Instead of commanding the corvids to serve her, he continued to subvert her, letting the birds choose who to fuel instead. Some chose poorly, but what Lloth didn't seem to notice was most were drawn to the other woman capable of drawing on corvid magic.

Lloth screeched something, but he couldn't make it

out. Too consumed with drawing power and redirecting the magic to his sister, he lost himself to the overwhelming sensation of the power coursing through his body. Sweat poured down his face. Hordes of corvids flooded into the grand hall. The Otherworld energy within him twisted and spiraled, aching to emerge, to be set free.

Raven's magic wound around the corvid energy in the room, including his own. It built and built until it became a tsunami of feral magic waiting to crash down and destroy everything in the room.

Raven screamed. Her body contorted. Bones snapped. Flesh compressed and expanded. Her stained shirt and shorts tore as her body ripped through them like paper. Feathers and scales sprouted. In an instant, her raven essence wiped away what remained of her human form, leaving a large bird in its place.

She towered over the men and women in the room.

"Holy fuck," he whispered.

Men and women screamed and ran from the courtyard. Some of the guards escaped with them, their heavy boots slapping the hard tile. Lloth's caomhnóir drew his sword and stepped forward.

Raven launched into the air and pumped her wings to move toward the Corvid Queen. Large gusts of Underworld air blasted past him.

"No," Lloth sneered. She turned toward his sister and raised her scythe, an evil smile spread across her face. She opened her mouth and mumbled a dark spell. The metal of her weapon glowed and pulsed with the swirling magic.

Raven pulled her wings in and dove.

Lloth threw her arms wide, shrieking ancient words.

Her personal guardian stepped up the dais.

No. Not today.

Bear called to the birds. He sent them his memories of Tasha and his love for the wily raven. The birds turned to the warrior as one. Hundreds of beady eyes focused on the man. Together, they launched from their perches and dove onto Lloth's caomhnóir, a deadly swarm of sharp beaks and talons. He screamed and thrashed at the birds, but it was futile. They stabbed him while Bear sang the dark and eerie call of corvids.

For Tasha.

Chapter Nineteen

"Sooner or later, everyone sits down to a banquet of consequences."

~ Robert Louis Stevenson

W hile Bear sang and lamented the loss of his shadow and the birds exacted revenge on his behalf, a loud commotion broke out on the dais where Lloth still chanted dark fae gibberish at his twin sister. The queen continued to pull on the corvid energy that surged in the room like a rising spring tide.

Lloth suddenly turned away from Raven, distracted

by what was happening on the stage. The shadows thinned. Cole appeared beside Lloth and the hilt of a dagger protruded from her chest.

"Traitor!" Lloth shrieked.

Before she could retaliate, Raven swooped down. Lloth flung her hands up and screamed, but nothing stopped Raven's momentum. She opened her enormous beak and clamped onto Lloth's head. The queen's skull jammed in her bill like a fragile sunflower seed.

Lloth thrashed and pummeled her fists against Raven's feathers.

His twin snapped her beak shut and chaos descended on the grand hall.

Metal rang as warriors and guards unsheathed their swords. Courtiers screeched like banshees and fled in fear, their footsteps thundered against the cold stonework. And Bear sat on his butt, still shackled and useless.

Raven shifted back to human form and fainted. He lurched forward, ready to stand, but a wave of nausea sat him back on his butt. He'd pulled too much power and now he couldn't even bum-scooch to where his sister lay to comfort her.

Luckily, it didn't appear as if he was needed. The two dark fae lords he feared would kill him last week cut down all the guards and soldiers brave enough to stay in the room. Seeing their ruthless efficiency did nothing to alleviate or remove his apprehension for them. Instead, he swayed where he sat while his mind bombarded him with questions. When would the fae notice him? When would they turn to cut him down, too?

And when had the second fae lord arrived?

Bear hadn't noticed anyone entering the courtyard before Raven shifted into a giant fucking bird other than the ache of magic as it pulsed through him.

At least he'd managed to help Raven by supplying her with magic. Bear took a deep breath and the waves of nausea subsided. At least he'd avenged Tasha.

Sort of.

Lloth's caomhnóir lay motionless on the ground in a pool of blood. A few ravens remained, hate-pecking at his body. As satisfying as the sight was in a sick twisted way, the man shouldn't have died so quickly from the bird attack. Something else must've killed him.

Bear looked over at Lloth's remains. His stomach turned again.

Get a hold of yourself, Crawford.

The sacred bond. Lloth had mentioned the guard was tied to her in a sacred bond of some sort. Her death must've caused his. Good riddance.

"Here." Chloe crouched beside him and unlocked the shackles. She cupped his face and peered into his eyes. "Are you okay?"

"I have no idea what just happened."

"I think your sister just kicked some ass."

He looked around the bloody room filled with dead bodies. "I've never been so proud."

Chloe laughed, and stood, pulling him with her.

"Come, we need to get you out of here before Cole or Bane remember they want to kill you, too."

Bane. That must be the name of the dark fae client he'd defied. The name sounded familiar. Bane. Dark fae lord. Bear's stomach sunk. Only one deadly fae lord that Bear knew of had that name. He knew the fae had been powerful when they met to discuss the job, but he hadn't realized how much. But surely this couldn't be a coincidence. "Bane..."

She nodded, probably seeing the exact moment he placed the name. "The Lord of War."

Bear Crawford was a dead man walking. "Why are you helping me?"

Chloe rolled her eyes. "For a smart guy, you certainly say some stupid shit sometimes." She tugged on his arm. "Let's go."

He shook his head. He was done with hiding, and he had nowhere to run. His disappearance had brought Raven into this mess and he couldn't afford the dark fae going after his family again because Bear was too scared to face the consequences. He didn't stand for much, but he would stand for his family. Any day. Any time. "I need to see this out."

She sighed and stared at the night sky above. "Fine. Let's go make sure your sister is okay."

They turned to find the Lord of fucking War squatting beside his sister. His deep voice echoed through the room. "Little Raven."

His sister had propped herself up to look around. Naked from shifting back to human form, blood covered her face and splattered her body. She was so pale and looked so lost, and a dark fae lord hovered beside her, imposing, armed and dragging a finger through a pool of blood like the sick fuck he was.

Bear lurched forward, but Chloe's hand on his arm tightened. She shook her head.

"What have you done?" Bane mused. His tone implied he didn't want or need an answer, which was for the best since his sister looked ready to pass out again.

Bear shrugged off Chloe's hand and stalked toward his sister.

The other dark fae lord, the Shadow Man named Cole finished wiping off his weapon and removed his cloak. He spread it over Raven to cover her shivering body, and the look the fae gave his sister...

Bear pulled up short and stared.

The big bad fae who'd stepped out of shadows in the vault, the man who'd kept Chloe locked in a box, the fae who'd cut down Lloth's guards as if he brushed aside annoying weeds on an overgrown forest path, the dark fae lord who embodied the word lethal and scared the crap out of Bear, looked at Raven with...tenderness?

Chloe walked up beside him, reached over and shut his mouth.

"Do we have a problem here?" Cole asked Bane.

"A problem? No. You've just handed me the solution." Bane chuckled and turned to leave. Though Bane hadn't glanced Bear's way once, Bear knew the fae lord hadn't forgotten him. An invisible weight pressed down on his shoulders. He'd have to answer for his betrayal.

"Wait!" Raven called out. "My brother? Spare him."

What the fuck, Rayray? Don't ask anything of a dark fae lord. Mom spent their entire childhoods outlining exactly why that wasn't a good idea. Why would she ask Bane to spare him, anyway? Him? The wayward brother who ghosted on his own family? Whose removal from her life caused her own power to weaken? He didn't deserve it. He didn't deserve her.

"You will owe me a favour," Bane said.

Bear couldn't let her do this. Just as she needed to clean up her own messes, he needed to answer for his. He shook his head. "I'm not worth it, Rayray."

"Done," Raven said without hesitation.

Bear groaned in unison with Cole. He looked over at the other man and met a gaze full of malice. Bear had stolen from him, but that look wasn't about the Claíomh Solais. This was all about Raven.

"Consider him safe from retribution," Bane said.

A deep sigh escaped Raven's lips and his love for his sister grew. She shouldn't have done it, but she'd bought him a second chance. She'd saved his life and he needed to make sure he didn't waste it.

"My mercy is payment for a favour owed." Bane chucked a lodestone at the floor and stepped into the portal that formed, quickly disappearing from their lives. At least for now.

"That was a mistake," Cole grumbled.

"Could you have kept Bear safe indefinitely from the Lord of War if he wanted him dead?" Raven said.

Cole's scowl was answer enough. "Come. I need to get you and Chloe to safety."

Oh, fuck that. Something inside him snapped. Drained from captivity and torture, exhausted from Lloth's magical manipulations, something hot and potent roared to life and took over his body. Nobody was taking Chloe away from him again. Without thinking about the consequences, without stopping to have a proper discussion, Bear launched himself at the Shadow Man with all his anger, frustration and confusion. "You can't have her!"

They hit the ground and rolled. Bear struck out and viciously jabbed the man's sides. Cole didn't hesitate to respond. They exchanged punches and jabs.

"She's my sister, you idiot." Cole punched Bear's stomach. "I was protecting her, not caging her."

"Oomph." The air from his lungs rushed out. Bear curled up and groaned. This guy was better than he was. And her brother? Fuck. That made sense. Bear had messed up again.

Cole continued to pound his fists into Bear's body. Why were they still fighting? Bear had stopped. He now covered up, moving back and forth to deflect as many of the blows as possible, looking for an opening to escape the rain of fists. They kept coming.

"Cole!" Raven and Chloe shrieked at the same time.

Cole stopped, his fist hovering in the air a few inches from Bear's face. He crouched over Bear and in unison, they both turned to find Chloe standing with her arms crossed, glaring at them. "That's enough."

In one swift movement, Cole stood and loomed over him. The moonlight from above played with the shadows of the man's face. His expression promised pain and suffering.

Bear scowled and slowly got to his feet. Pain shot through his body, but not as much as it should have. Cole had pulled some of his punches, hitting Bear to make a point more than to cause damage.

Bear brushed off the dirt from his skin. Blood streaked his chest and the paste used to draw the runes had smeared, making war-like stripes along his torso.

Raven gaped at him with a "what the fuck?" expression plastered on her face. They were so alike in many ways.

Yeah, what the fuck? Why had he launched himself at Cole? Why had he reacted so violently to the idea of Chloe being taken away? Bear knew the answer.

"I love Chloe," he announced, the words ringing true despite how absurd it must sound to everyone, including his former self. "You can't take her from me."

Chloe sighed and their gazes met. Yes. He said what he said, and surprisingly, she wasn't running away or mocking him. Instead, the black of her eyes bled out to cover the white, and her mouth parted. Power rolled off her and she glowed, emitting light like a beacon. And like a moth, he wanted to go to the flames. He wanted to snatch her up in his arms, find a safe place for them to be alone, and revel in the heat of her power.

Cole's eyes narrowed. "Like I said, I'm her brother. I have no intention of fighting you, nor any plans to harm my sister."

"Why'd you keep hitting me then?"

Cole's lips spread into a nasty smile. "Those shots were for your sister."

Okay, Bear deserved that. He tore his gaze away from Chloe to study his sister. She looked ready to fall over. He really was an asshole. He took three giant steps and held his twin in his arms. Their magic pinged against each other. Her spring rain scent mixed with mischief wrapped around them and the dark energy inside him hummed. He spoke into her hair, his voice muffled. "Rayray."

"Brother Bear." She relaxed in his arms and squeezed him back. Everything was going to be okay.

"You're a shitty brother," Cole said somewhere behind him. The urge to punch the dark fae lord returned.

Bear reluctantly stepped away from Raven to face Chloe's brother. As much as this man scared and pissed him off at the same time, Bear couldn't deny Cole was right. "I am. I hadn't realized how much I hurt her or myself with my absence. I will make it up to her."

"You better." The shadows drew around Cole, surrounding him like a liquid threat.

Bear straightened and pulled his shoulders back. Oh, it was like that, was it?

"How about instead of posturing with one another, you take us home?" Chloe stood with her hands on her hips. "I want to scrub off your psycho ex's doodles, and Bear's sister looks like she's about to fall over."

They all turned to Raven. Her body went limp, but instead of falling to the ground, bands of shadows shot out from the corners of the room and caught her. Huh. Cole might hate him, but the fae had feelings for his sister.

Bear didn't know how to begin processing that. The man was a walking dagger—slick and stunning in a lethal way, but dangerous and sharp to touch—but none of the barely contained malice was directed at his sister.

Cole gathered Raven in his arms, supported by the bands of shadow and looked down at her possessively.

Bear suddenly felt uncomfortable, as if he was intruding on a personal moment and his sister wasn't even conscious. He shifted his weight and cleared his throat.

As if only now realizing he had an audience, Cole looked up at Chloe and Bear standing side by side. He scowled at Bear before turning to Chloe. "Shall we go?"

"Yes, but you're taking both of us." She reached down and clasped Bear's hand. "Together."

Warmth spread through Bear's chest and he squeezed her hand back. That was the best thing he'd heard all week.

Epilogue

"There is never a time or place for true love. It happens accidentally, in a heartbeat, in a single flashing, throbbing moment."

~ Sarah Dessen

Bear threw his keys on the kitchen counter and watched Chloe walk around his apartment—his real one, not the safe house. Though the building was decrepit and the street run down, his place was clean and well furnished. The only thing missing was Tasha's indignant croak. She hated when he left her outside.

His heart dropped.

"No personal items." Chloe turned and frowned.

"I have a cat." He rounded his shoulders and shoved his hands in his pockets. "And a picture of me and Raven."

"Of course, you do."

What did she mean by that? More of that soulmate crap? He couldn't deny he had a connection with his sister and it strengthened in her presence, but he wasn't so sure about the whole two sides to the same coin thing. "You could've told me the Shadow Man was your brother. I would've returned you to him."

"That's precisely why I didn't."

Huh? If he'd contacted Cole and bartered for her return in exchange for sparing his life, he would've only had to worry about Bane.

And he never would've gotten to know Chloe.

"I was curious to see what you'd do and what we could become," Chloe continued.

"We?" Why did his chest expand with warmth and lightness like that? Why did she seem to have this power over him?

"I heard what you said earlier, Pretty Boy." She folded her arms. "We."

He scratched his head. "Yeah, about that..."

She cocked her head, a small smile playing on her lips like she was in on some inside joke. "Did you not mean it?"

"No. Yes. I don't know. I've never said that to anyone before. I'm not sure if it's true. I barely know you. How can it be true? That's weird, don't you think? Too quick."

Kissa chose that moment to saunter out of his bedroom. The cat despised his sister and Bear always suspected her hatred stemmed from jealousy. Kissa never liked any of the women he brought home.

The cat continued to strut through the apartment like she worked her own personal runway, tail straight in the air. When she reached Chloe's leg, Bear braced for the hell-beast to freak out.

Instead, after one sniff, Kissa rubbed her cheek on Chloe's jeans. A loud purr erupted from her chest.

Bear rocked back on his heels. He didn't believe in fate or signs from above, but his cat and Tasha both told him the same thing in their own way—they liked Chloe—and that meant something to him.

He dragged his gaze away from Kissa to look up at Chloe. He found her amused smile gone. The crinkles around her eyes softened and she walked over to where he stood by some overripe bananas. "Some things in life defy logical explanations."

Though he understood at some level what she meant, he still didn't trust the potency of their connection. He'd never been one to fall hard or fast. In fact, he wasn't one to fall at all. "What do you suggest?"

Instead of answering, she slid her hands up his shoulders and neck to grip the back of his head and pulled him down for a kiss. Her lips pressed against his and her magic, light and bright, coiled around him. Warmth spread through his body and tingled his toes.

She tasted like sugar and naughty promises whispered at midnight.

He held her in his arms and kissed her back. She felt right like this, with him. He didn't know what romantic love was. He loved his family, of course, but that was different. That wasn't the same thing as love for a partner. He'd take it slow and figure things out. He didn't deserve her—that was for certain—but she didn't seem to mind.

Sure, this was new, and uncomfortable. But for the first time in a long time, he had hope.

~The End~

Did you enjoy reading The Call of Corvids? Please help this author out and tell someone or leave a review. Your support is much appreciated.

If you haven't read the Raven Crawford books yet and want to know more of the story, start with
Conspiracy of Ravens
(*A Raven Crawford Story, Book 1*),
a full-length novel by J. C. McKenzie.

GLOSSARY OF TERMS

Anam cara: Roughly translated from dark fae to English, Anam Cara means "soul friend." It is a deeply felt, eternal fae bond that allows two souls to flow together in a way that transcends time, place and definition. The anam cara bond allows souls to access each other's strength, power and magic. According to John O'Donohue, "when you are blessed with an anam cara...you have arrived at the most sacred place: home." (*Anam Cara: A book of Celtic Wisdom*, 998).

Caomhnóir: Guardian who is blood sworn to protect fae nobility.

Dark fae: Any fae from any of the realms within the Underworld. They are called "dark" fae because of their eyes and hue of their magic. The pupil of a dark fae eyes appears to "bleed out," when in fact it's the iris that turns black and spreads to cover the whites of the eyes. This is caused during intense emotion or when accessing vast amounts of power. Dark fae are compatible with humans and have a wide range of human physical traits, though they are always attractive. Dark fae are the most feared by mortals due to their ability to blend in with regs, eagerness to exploit mortal weaknesses and willingness to venture into the Mortal Realm for their own personal gain.

Mortal: Any inhabitant of the Mortal Realm. Note: All entities of all the realms can be killed, but this term is reserved for anyone who is not an Other. Used as a derogatory slur by Others.

Other: Any inhabitant NOT from the Mortal Realm. Any inhabitant from the Realm of Light, the Underworld or the Shadow Realm. Mortal, but not a mortal.

Reg: A "regular" human being from the Mortal Realm without any supernatural powers or skills.

Underworld: An Other realm, often in direct conflict with the Realm of Light. Contains multiple, smaller realms, such as the realms of War and Lust.

ACKNOWLEDGEMENTS

This story originally appeared in an even shorter version as a part of a box set called *Heart of a Phoenix*. This project was dedicated to raising funds for those negatively impacted by the Australian bushfires in January 2020. I dedicated that short story, and this version as well, to Mirren Hogan, who was one of many to lose a home in these fires. My heart goes out to Mirren, and I hope rebuilding will bring her a sense of peace in this chaotic time.

Thank you to Margo Bond Collins for inviting me to participate in the box set and great cause.

Thank you to my fabulous beta readers, Jo-Ann Carson, Brianne Melnyk, Maureen Bonatch, Karilyn Bentley, Nicole Flockton and Wendy P.

Thank you to Lara Parker, my extraordinary editor and DP, my proof-reader at Book Nook Nuts.

I love how supportive the writing community and how everyone comes together to help others in need.

Thank you to my friends and family for their continued love and support.

And last, but certainly not least, thank you to you, the reader, for supporting me and enjoying the stories I create.

About the Author

J. C. McKenzie is a book-loving, gumboot-wearing, unapologetic science geek. She's the author of the Carus Series, the Obsidian Flame Series and the Raven Crawford Series. Born and raised on the West Coast, J. C. sets the majority of her books in the Lower Mainland of British Columbia, Canada. She writes urban fantasy and paranormal romance with sassy heroines and brutish, alpha-type men.

Visit her at www.jcmckenzie.ca

Amazon: www.amazon.com/author/jcmckenzie
Blog: jcmckenzie.blogspot.ca
Goodreads: www.goodreads.com/JCMcKenzie
Twitter: twitter.com/JC_McKenzie
Facebook: www.facebook.com/j.c.mckenzie.author
Instagram: www.instagram.com/j.c.mckenzie